Isabella's Book

Alison Mukherjee

For GKG

With sincere thanks to Rachel

Cover photography, Kevin Ward

Cover design, Pippa Greenwood

ALSO BY ALISON MUKHERJEE

Nirmal Babu's Bride

An Untimely Frost

O heavenly Muse…
Inspire life in my wit,
my thoughts upraise,
My verse ennoble,
and forgive the thing,
If fictions light I mix
with truth divine,
And fill these lines with
other praise than thine.

Torquato Tasso

CHAPTER 1

2007

The little leather pouch was drab and shabby, though Tibby thought she could see traces of the original colour. It was fastened with a type of button she hadn't seen before, made from compacted cloth and presumably quite old. The lining was a nice surprise. Grey silk with coral-coloured flowers. And nestling inside was a little book. Really little, not much more than two inches by four and almost as thick as it was wide.

A delicate gold filigree design spread out across the black leather cover then spilled over onto the polished page ends. The facing pages were decorated with the marble effect common in old books, and the colours, magenta, blue and orange, were still bright. The title page declared the tiny volume to be the Holy Bible printed in London by John Field, Printer to Parliament, 1653.

Altogether a nice object. Lovely to look at, satisfying to hold and more than three and a half centuries old. But was it commercial? Could she make a profit from it? She had to be hard-headed and focus on profit if she was going to have her own stall one day. That was the idea. Her project. The pre-retirement guru said you should always have a project on the go, especially during winter.

'Sweet isn't it?' The stallholder was watching her. 'Family bible. House clearance. Same box as a rather nice collection of teaspoons.' He turned away to serve another customer.

Tibby glanced at the other items on the stall. Postcards from every seaside resort in the country, collections of vinyl records and beer mats, vintage cookery books and knitting patterns. None of it interested her. She put the little book back on the table and wandered down to the other end of the hall where the stalls were devoted entirely to items from a single category; porcelain, glass or jewellery.

The men and women behind the tables watched her suspiciously and moved closer to their precious collections. More like security guards than salesmen. She enquired about some tiny coffee cups. Copeland Spode, Chinese Rose pattern. The price was much too high and the seller wasn't prepared to bargain. She moved on to glassware and checked the price tag on an Edwardian cut glass carafe. Way beyond her budget and quite impractical, she'd be certain to break it. As she walked away Tibby could almost hear the sighs of relief behind her.

There was something very appealing about that little bible. She went back for a second look. Damn! Someone else had spotted it, a tall man in a leather jacket. She hovered close by, pretending to be tempted by a watercolour of the Swiss Alps. Good, he was moving on to another stall. She grabbed the book quickly before anyone else noticed it.

There were two handwritten inscriptions at the front. That explained why the stallholder called it a family bible. The first inscription was written in small, neat letters with only a few loops and twiddles:

Isabella Paitson's Book
Given (by her Mother)
in the year 1774.

Tibby could just picture Isabella, a young woman not yet mature, taking care not to smudge the letters as the quill pen scratches the surface of the page. She pauses to review what she's written then squeezes in the bracketed words as an afterthought.

And on the following page, bolder and more elaborate with copious twirls and flourishes:

Peter Moser's Book,
Given him by Isabella Thompson,
late Paitson, this 28th:
day of June 1827.

Peter is a man of substance sitting at a mahogany desk. Relaxed and confident. The pen glides over the page recording in detail the transfer of ownership as he proudly adds his signature to Isabella's.

Tibby recalled how, as a child, she went through a phase of refusing to write her name. She remembered exactly what prompted it. It was the day after her mother got married and Tibby's stepfather was introducing his new family to a neighbour.

'I'd like you to meet my wife,' he said. Tibby's mother smiled dutifully and stepped forward to shake hands. 'And this is the wife's brother's little girl.' He gestured to Tibby to shake hands as her mother had just done. But Tibby didn't move, even when her mother gave her a sharp nudge.

The wife's brother's little girl? Uncle David her father? Impossible! That would mean her mother used to be married to Uncle David and Tibby was sure you couldn't marry your own brother. She waited for her stepfather to correct himself and when he didn't she stared at her mother, who, far from putting things straight, continued to grin stupidly at the neighbour.

When she was older Tibby realised her stepfather had only been trying to preserve his wife's dignity. He couldn't very well say, 'This is the wife's illegitimate daughter.' But at the time Tibby was full of shame. Her surname was the same as Uncle David's and she refused to write it.

Looking at Isabella and Peter's inscriptions, Tibby was gripped by an overwhelming urge to find out who they were. Far more interesting than trying to make money out of antiques. It shouldn't be too difficult either. Everyone was doing it, tracing their ancestors. There were plenty of online resources and Paitson and Moser were both unusual names which should make it easier.

The stallholder was enjoying a mug of tea with the woman on the neighbouring stall. He noticed Tibby still holding the little bible and came over.

'You going to buy that?'

'It depends on the price.' Tibby thought she'd better make a show of bargaining although she'd already made up her mind.

He sucked air between his teeth. 'I'll let you have it for a fiver.'

'I'll take it.' She took out her purse.

'I kept the wrapping paper. You can take it if you want.'

He rummaged under the table and handed her a crumpled ball of brown paper, soft and limp from a hundred foldings and unfoldings. The address label was torn but Tibby could just make out "Moser & Sons, Solicitors, Kendal" embossed along the bottom edge. A few red shards were all that remained of the wax seal. The sight of them brought back the smell of hot sealing wax and the satisfaction of pressing a stamp into the red blob, quickly before it hardened.

'Yes, I'll take this as well. Thanks.' Tibby wrapped the little book in the brown paper and slipped it into her bag.

She'd only been home five minutes when the phone rang. It was Lottie, her sister, or half-sister to be precise. Lottie wanted to hear all about the Antiques and Collectables Sale.

'It was okay.' Tibby wriggled out of her coat, arm by arm, without letting go of the receiver. 'The usual stalls. Nothing particularly exciting. There weren't many people there. I'm not sure why.'

'Because of the weather probably,' Lottie said. 'Did

you buy anything?'

'I know this sounds odd but I bought a bible. A beautiful, miniature bible with its own pouch. Printed in Oliver Cromwell's time.' Tibby caught sight of herself in the hall mirror and attempted to fluff up her lifeless hair.

'I'm not sure what to say! Is there much demand for antique bibles?' Lottie was teasing.

'I know. It does sound a bit strange. But it's not just any old bible. It's got two inscriptions in it, Isabella Paitson and Peter Moser. That's why I bought it, because of the writing.'

'And you want to find out who Isabella and Peter were?' Lottie knew her sister inside out. 'Do you have anything else to go on, apart from the names?'

'Two dates.' Tibby pulled the little book from her bag. 'Isabella's mother gave the book to her in 1774, then Isabella passed it on to Peter in 1827.'

'I think you'd better sign up for evening classes in Family History. You'll meet some interesting people.'

Lottie was always trying to get Tibby to go out and meet people. She had the idea Tibby needed looking after now that she'd retired. It was the other way round when they were children, Lottie depended upon Tibby. If she fell and hurt herself she wanted Tibby to kiss it better. When their mother sat down to read a story, Lottie would snatch the book and scramble onto Tibby's knee. And Lottie insisted on Tibby being with her the first day she went to school.

Tibby's stepfather said Lottie had imprinted on Tibby like a duckling. Which could be true because Tibby's face peering over the side of the cot was one of the first things Lottie's eyes focused on when the foetal mist cleared. Tibby didn't mind. She was pleased to have someone who adored her.

That night Tibby took Isabella's book upstairs with her and examined it in bed, propped up on pillows. She always had plenty of pillows. She held the little book by the spine and shook hard as she did before returning a library book, in case she'd used something important as a bookmark and forgotten to remove it.

A clump of hair fell onto the duvet. Tibby spread the separate strands out across her palm for a better look. They came from at least two different heads. Isabella and her husband? Isabella's children, or Peter Moser's? A detective investigating a crime would order samples to be sent off to the lab for genetic tests.

It felt strangely intimate to be holding part of someone who lived so long ago. Tibby imagined she could hear Isabella calling to her down the centuries, 'You've touched my hair, now you have to find out who I am.' She wrapped the hair in tissue paper and slipped it into her jewellery box.

CHAPTER 2

1768

Andrew Paitson was overjoyed when he heard Miss Ridley had bequeathed him Rawridding in her will, indeed he could scarcely believe his good fortune for he had known and loved the place most of his life.

As a young lad he often accompanied his father on business trips to Dentdale and, however weary and hungry, before returning home they would toil up the steep lane to Rawridding farmhouse. Miss Ridley was well known for miles around as a provider of loans and mortgages, and Andrew's father deemed it important to maintain cordial relations lest he require her services one day.

Andrew was a little scared at first, for Miss Ridley wore her hair cut short and drank gin and swore oaths just like her farm hands, but she was also kind; while she and his father conversed, Andrew was dispatched to the kitchen for a heel of bread which he stuffed into his pocket so that both hands were free to haul himself up into the huge sycamore which grew behind the farmhouse. Spread out below, the building resembled an owl in flight, a large south facing porch protruded to the fore in the manner of a head while to the rear a broad service block formed the tail.

Sitting astride a branch, his arms and legs laced with scratches from bark and twigs, Andrew chewed his bread and watched the breeze send clouds tumbling across the sky while their shadows played Catch Me over the fells. When it was time to leave, Miss Ridley handed him an apple or a wedge of cheese to sustain him on the homeward journey.

After his father's death, Andrew continued to make regular trips to Dentdale to purchase knitted goods, and always found time to pay his respects to Miss Ridley. Now his attentiveness was rewarded; a spinster with no close relatives, she had chosen to leave him the sturdy farmhouse set in the midst of the fells, a house which in Andrew's estimation was the perfect place to bring up a family. However, when he announced the good news to Margaret, his wife, it was evident she did not share his enthusiasm.

'Are there any people of our kind living nearby?' she inquired. 'I mean to say, people I can mix with, who have taste and good manners.'

'Indeed there are,' said Andrew who had never considered the matter. 'I'm sure you'll find the perpetual curate's wife has perfect manners, as do the doctor's two sisters. But don't forget, my dear, though the villagers may not be our social equals, our livelihood depends upon their labour.'

'That's very true and I'm grateful for it.' Margaret, duly chastened, altered the line of her attack. 'But what about the children's schooling? There's no shortage of people ready to take pupils here in Kirkby Kendal, but will we find a governess in Dent?'

'There's a grammar school standing within the churchyard.' Andrew was relieved to have a solution to hand. 'A worthy establishment for William to attend. And if we can't find anyone to instruct the girls, why then we'll teach them ourselves!'

But Margaret was not so easily silenced. The people of Dent were known for their rebellious nature, she said. Their son, William, whose mind was particularly sensitive, would be led astray.

'Come with me and see for yourself,' Andrew proposed when he saw reason alone would not convince her, 'then you'll understand.'

He took her to the place where fells to the west meet dales to the east, an area known locally as North Lord's Land. They stood side by side in the yard to the front of the farmhouse, he tall and lean with hair that grew low on his forehead, she with her head held high but of gentle demeanour. Before them, the ground dropped steeply down to the River Dee and beyond that to South Lord's Land, while to the rear the land swept upwards to the fells beyond the house.

'Did you ever see a sight more delightful?' enquired Andrew.

'So pretty!' said Margaret.

In truth she found the landscape crude and the house lacking in refinement, but, observing how much her husband loved the place, she dropped her objections. And so it was that Andrew Paitson moved from Kirkby Kendal to Dentdale with his wife and five children.

Nancy, the firstborn, was generously endowed with common sense and devoted her time to helping her mother about the house. Next came William, a lad of slender build and lacking in strength, who spent many solitary hours wandering the fells and rarely spoke, and when he did the words struggled to pass his lips.

William was followed by Meg, a stalwart soul whose misfortune it was to be slow of wit, clumsy of hand, and to bear the scars of small pox on her face. By contrast, her younger sister Sarah's auburn hair and emerald eyes drew the admiration of all who saw her. Last but not least came Isabella, who possessed a pleasing countenance and a cheerful disposition.

One Midsummer's Eve, Andrew gathered the older children. 'I have a surprise for you,' he said. 'Tomorrow I'll wake you early, well before dawn, and you must dress in your woollens, though it's summer.'

'What is the surprise?' asked Meg.

'Silly!' said Nancy. 'If Papa told you what it was, well then it wouldn't be a surprise any more.'

'Please can I come too?' Isabella took her father's hand and looked up into his face.

'Not this time, Bella. You're too young and would quickly tire. I'll take you when you're a little older.'

But Isabella was determined not to be excluded from the expedition; she rose part way through the night and dressed herself and went downstairs and waited by the door so that the others might not embark on the surprise without her. Observing her eagerness, Andrew relented and included her in the party.

In spite of Margaret's protests they set off while it was still quite dark and, keeping close together, climbed the fell behind the house. Isabella was soon out of breath and her knees ached but she kept up with the others till they reached the summit. Shivering with cold she stood and watched in wonder as the sky first lightened, then flushed coral peach, while the glowing circle of the sun crept over the horizon colouring the clouds.

The air was filled with the song of skylarks while shades of amber, sage and unpolished gold suffused the land beneath. The sight touched Andrew's heart like the joy of Easter anthems after forty days Lententide or the sad sweetness of poetry recited with due sentiment. Isabella, holding tight to his hand, could scarcely believe the beauty of it. She watched their shadows stretch out like giants as they retraced their steps.

Isabella possessed more than her share of wits and was always eager to learn. She discovered a place near the river where wild herbs grew in abundance, and filled her lap and brought them home and when Andrew returned that night she was waiting for him in the yard.

'See, Papa, I have drawn the shapes of the leaves and flowers but I need to write their names and properties.' She jumped from one foot to the other in her excitement.

'Not now, Bella,' Margaret intervened. 'Your father is tired, he will call you when he is rested.' Then, seeing the stains on Isabella's gown, Margaret forbade her to venture beyond the yard until she was old enough to take proper care of her clothing.

Isabella obeyed and did not go into the fields the following day, but searched under every stone and piece of rotting wood about the yard and collected beetles and spiders and held them in one hand while she copied their shape and markings with the other, then set them free.

After he had eaten, Andrew examined the sketches and did his best to name them. She was such an eager pupil! Sometimes when the night sky was clear, he fetched Isabella from her bed, too impatient to wait for her to put on her shoes, and carried her swathed in a rug into the yard. He lifted her onto his shoulders and pointed to the stars.

'See, Bella, three stars close together. They form Orion the Hunter's belt. Look beneath and you'll see his feet.'

'Yes! And he's holding a sword. Who is he chasing, Papa?' Isabella was fully awake now and straining to distinguish one star from another.

'Taurus the Bull. Do you see his horns? Here, to this side. And on his shoulder Pleiades, the Seven Sisters.'

Forgetting Isabella was perched on his shoulders, Andrew used both hands to illustrate his lesson so that she must cling on if she was not to lose her balance. She could not always trace the shapes of the constellations, but the names sounded to her like magic spells and she committed them to memory.

It was left to Margaret to oversee the children's book learning, it being impossible to secure the services of a governess. While they were very young Margaret performed this task admirably, but as they grew older, she lacked the time and knowledge to provide what was needful for a sound education. Isabella yearned for a teacher to satisfy her curiosity, and begged her father to bring back any written material he could lay his hands on, for her to peruse.

It was evident to all that Margaret was increasingly

unhappy. When she dressed the children's hair, she did so roughly, with impatience, rather than her former gentleness; she was vexed when baby Agnes cried and scolded her, which Isabella thought somewhat unjust because crying was the thing babies did best; and worst of all Margaret complained to Alice, the household servant, that the master was forever going away, leaving his family unprotected and alone at night, which everyone knew was the kind of thing one should never say within earshot of servants.

So Isabella was not surprised when, lying awake one night, she overheard her mother present her father with a list of reasons why they should leave Dentdale.

'I saw Sarah strut around the yard yesterday,' Margaret said when Andrew was comfortably seated with a glass of port. 'Samuel's sons were gawping and competing which should speak to her first. '

'I can see why.' Andrew laughed. 'Sarah's the beauty of the bunch. No wonder she attracts attention!' In spite of this casual rejoinder, Andrew was in truth disturbed at the thought of his daughter parading before any young men, let alone the sons of his farmhand.

Margaret fetched the shoes warming by the fire, Andrew's favourite pair because the leather bulged to accommodate the precise shape of his bunions and was flattened around the heel so he need not push his feet right inside. She tried again.

'William lacks the stamina to undertake the daily journey to Dent,' she said. 'The boy hasn't attended school these two weeks. His education suffers.'

'My son is a mystery to me,' Andrew sighed, 'and will remain so whether we live here or in the town.' He could make no sense of William, who kept his own counsel and was afraid to meet his father's eye. Indeed there were times when Andrew looked upon his son with distaste, though he was ashamed to own it.

14

'Nancy has entered her seventeenth year,' said Margaret, coming to the point. 'Have you considered whether it might be time for us to leave Rawridding for her sake, and for the future happiness of all our children?'

Isabella did not know which of her parents was in the right, but she wished they would settle the question rapidly.

'I have considered it, my dear.' Andrew stared into the restless, hungry flames which sent shadows leaping up the walls. 'In fact I've spent hours deliberating the question.'

'And have you arrived at a conclusion?' Margaret asked when she could be patient no longer.

Isabella squeezed her eyes tight shut and refrained from breathing.

'I conclude that you are right, my dear,' Andrew said, realising he had no choice but to surrender. 'It's best for us to leave this valley and return to Kirkby Kendal, as soon as it can be arranged.'

Isabella opened her eyes. So it was settled!

Over the coming days Margaret regaled her son and daughters with colourful descriptions of town life and Isabella was soon enchanted by the prospect of removal to Kirkby Kendal. She would have friends in the town, real friends. The children in the stories she read had friends with whom they shared secrets. Family was all very well but you knew to a great extent what they were going to say before they said it; friends would have different ideas and might surprise you.

The day before their departure Isabella and Nancy were busy wrapping the porcelain in strips of cloth ready to be packed, by their mother, in a large deal box fetched down from the parlour loft by Samuel. A china shepherdess slipped from Isabella's hand and landed, by good fortune, on the table and therefore did not break.

'Clumsy!' Nancy scolded. 'Try to keep your mind on

what you're doing.'

'I'm so excited my fingers refuse to behave themselves,' explained Isabella, full of remorse.

'Then you had better stop,' Margaret laughed, 'and go to Fowl Field to see if your sisters have finished with the hens. Take Aggie with you.'

Hearing this, Agnes left off playing with the dolls' house and hid herself from head to foot in her mother's skirts.

'I won't go! I want to stay with you, Mamma,' she squealed.

'I'll pick you an apple, the reddest on the tree,' Isabella promised. She approached Margaret's bunched up skirts and tickled her sister through the cloth. Agnes began to giggle.

Isabella had discovered this was the way to deal with Agnes when she was peevish, that is to coax laughter from her. When Meg was out of sorts, it was best to say nothing and leave her to her own devices and soon enough her good nature would reassert itself. But if you did the same with Sarah, you would end up playing servant to her queen for evermore, which was not good for either of you, as Mamma so often remarked.

Agnes soon emerged happily from her cocoon and she and Isabella set out hand in hand across the yard, where Samuel and his two sons were loading household goods and furniture into a large cart, ably assisted by Joseph Thompson, carrier and supplier of said cart, a man willing to turn his hand to anything.

The oak chest and set of mahogany drawers were in place; Samuel and Joseph were now arranging the more delicate pieces in such a manner that they would not work free on the uneven roads.

The loading was, in theory, taking place under Andrew's supervision. However, Isabella could see Andrew's attention was largely given over to the negotiations he was carrying on with a business acquaintance. Observing Samuel struggle with the walnut writing bureau, Andrew broke off to castigate his farmhand.

'Pox take you, Samuel. How many more times should I tell you? Can you not see the best position for the bureau?'

'I can, Master. But my best position differs to some degree from thy best position. Now if you were to give over talking to this gentleman and step up here and show us what you mean.' Samuel untied his neckchief of homespun linsey and rubbed it over his face and neck.

Joseph leaned against the set of drawers, opened his snuffbox and waited with interest to see how such straight talking by a peasant would be received. One glance at her father's face told Isabella he was not angry at Samuel for speaking his mind, indeed he considered Samuel's suggestion sound common sense, and was about to fall in with it when Alice, Margaret's maidservant, blocked his way. Alice was not afraid of Papa and Isabella wondered what would transpire.

'Pardon me for saying so, but I've yet to meet a man could give his attention to two different things at one and the same time,' Alice said. 'What's best, Master, is for you to take the young gentleman here inside, and leave me to see to Samuel's loading.' Without waiting for a reply she hitched her skirts clear of her iron-shod wooden clogs, climbed into the cart and immediately began issuing orders, much to Samuel's discomfort and Joseph's entertainment. Andrew winked at Isabella, then set off obediently towards the house with his business associate in tow.

Meanwhile Isabella and Agnes continued on their way to the small, misshapen plot known as Fowl Field. It was Alice's duty to shut the birds up in the lopsided henhouse which stood hard up against the boundary wall, but today

Alice was otherwise occupied and Sarah and Meg were charged with the task.

'Mamma sent me to see how you're getting on,' Isabella said, although she could tell from their glum expressions they were not getting on at all well.

'If only Meg had shut the door when she was supposed to.' Sarah flopped down on a patch of grass which was threadbare from ceaseless scratching by beak and claw.

'I wasn't supposed to shut it,' Meg replied indignantly, and collapsed at Sarah's side. 'Not until they were all inside. And they weren't all inside.'

Isabella sat with her sisters and watched Agnes chase the hens, some black as coal, others white speckled with grey, round the field. The birds clucked their complaints at the rude disturbance. Someone was shouting in the yard and the sound of barking drifted up from one of the farms in the valley below. The sun sank slowly in the sky, taking with it the hint of warmth.

After a spell Isabella suggested they renew their efforts which, she pointed out, had more chance of success now they had an extra pair of hands to assist. The suggestion was accepted, and Isabella and Meg drove the hens, squawking and fluttering, towards the henhouse, but when Sarah opened the door to admit the last few, those already inside pushed their way out. The disheartened sisters once more spread themselves on the grass.

'A handful of grain would do it. Lay some trails towards the hut and throw the rest inside. They'll come willingly for grain.'

The sisters looked round in surprise, wondering who dispensed this piece of advice, and saw a fair-haired lad, of slight build and serious demeanour, sitting astride the gate swinging his legs. His coat was over-large so that only the tips of his fingers protruded from the sleeves, and his breeches reached well below his knee.

'Who says so?' Meg regarded the stranger with suspicion.

'Someone what knows about animals and birds,' he replied.

'Does this someone have a name?'

The boy identified himself as Isaac, son of Joseph, the driver and supplier of the cart that was now standing in the yard.

'What does a boy who lives in the town know about fowl?' Meg scoffed.

'Everyone in Kirkland keeps hens!' said Isaac, amazed at such ignorance. 'A body cannot sleep past dawn for the crowing of cocks on all sides.'

Isabella admired the way he sat quietly watching them before speaking up, which itself was a bold thing to do especially as he had never met them before. She sensed the boy knew what he was talking about and was not merely showing off.

Isabella was right. Isaac knew that if you wanted to work with bird or beast you must think like they think; imagine you are a hen or a horse and you will immediately understand how to handle hens or horses. Isaac also knew the capacity to imagine yourself an animal depended on close observation and sensitivity, which was not the same as simply being amongst animals. Some men spent their lives working with horses but did not understand horses at all.

'I think we should do as Isaac says.' Isabella winked at Isaac like a boy might wink, only with more charm.

Isaac responded with a slow smile which gradually spread over his face, puckering his cheeks, stretching the skin across his nose and making his eyes disappear altogether. Isabella thought anyone with a smile like that would make a very good friend.

The sisters debated the matter and at last Meg agreed they should put Isaac's advice to the test. Accordingly,

Isabella ran off towards the house, to fetch a pocketful of grain.

Sarah leaned against the wall and fixed Isaac with her emerald eyes. When he failed to respond she walked back and forth across the little field, swinging her hips and tossing her head, but Isaac showed no interest. He pulled a wedge of rye bread from his pocket and chewed methodically, keeping his eyes fixed on the path by which Isabella left and therefore by which he anticipated she would soon return.

CHAPTER 3

1768

Isabella woke early next morning and went immediately into the yard but the cart was already gone for Andrew had dispatched Joseph and Samuel soon after dawn. It was his plan to allow the heavy laden vehicle time to contend with the series of steep inclines which beset the road to Kirkby Kendal; the family would leave a little later in the carriage and soon catch up.

While Andrew attended to the handful of villagers come to bid him farewell, Margaret issued final instructions to Alice, who was to travel independently. Margaret then climbed up and settled herself amongst the children who were pressed together in the carriage like fleeces in a woolpack. Andrew seated himself on the box and the carriage finally began the descent to the valley floor.

'Wait! Papa, please!' cried Isabella as the farmhouse gradually receded from sight. 'I have to get down.'

'Why, Bella?' Andrew turned his head to catch her words. 'What have you forgotten?'

'I forgot to say goodbye to the house!'

'We can't go back.' Margaret said. 'You must fancy yourself saying goodbye.'

So Isabella whispered her farewell to the rectangular stone fireplace in the west wing where she warmed her hands on winter nights; to the rear room which smelt of damp clothes and melted dripping, where she once saw Alice sit on Samuel's knee like a child; to the open staircase and panelled landing leading to the bedroom where she and her sisters held hands when lightening seared the sky, and storms driving across the fells, threatened to lift the roof.

After some time, the road left the valley and became a series of steep ascents followed by shorter descents.

Isabella was distressed to see how their horse strained against the weight of the carriage and happily climbed down and walked alongside until she reached the summit, then scrambled back inside. Andrew showed her how to apply the chock to slow the wheels as the carriage rolled down the other side.

As the road gained height so the trees fell away and everything was wild and barren. Isabella thought the turf, stretched taut across the surrounding hills with no slack or generosity, pale and insipid compared to the rich colours of the valley. A little further, and Andrew pointed to clusters of reeds warning of marshy ground. This was Lilymere Tarn, where rumour had it the Bonnie Prince's army buried a chest of gold. Isabella imagined the weary Highlanders digging pits, reluctant to abandon the treasure but compelled to do so by aching bodies, unable any longer to bear its weight.

The inclines in the road now grew gentler and the ridges of the surrounding hills smoother. Neglected hedges with broad trunks coated in emerald green moss, edged the road. Isabella looked up to see the overgrown branches clasp hands above her head to form a tunnel.

As their carriage crested a small rise, she was surprised to spy Joseph's wagon stationary in the road ahead.

'Take Agnes in your lap,' Andrew whispered to Margaret. 'And keep the other children quiet.'

'Robbers?' Margaret's lips barely moved. 'Don't put up a fight. I'd rather they took our valuables than see you injured.'

Margaret signalled to the children to keep absolutely silent. She knew of passengers beaten with staves and left for dead at the roadside, and even worse, had heard rumours of young maidens ravished and children stolen and sold to work as slaves in the households of the aristocracy.

Isabella was frightened but at the same time curious. In her experience when she understood something, she ceased to fear it; she had been fearful hearing Papa and his friends talk about "unrest in the Colonies", but when she saw where the Colonies were on the map and heard the reason for the restlessness, her fear quickly dissipated.

So in the present case, Isabella longed to ask a highwayman face to face what it was that made him do such wicked things when all the while he knew, if he were caught, he would be sent to the gallows. She had seen pictures of Dick Turpin and Jack Sheppard and other highwaymen, and thought them more dashing than dastardly; so it was with a fleeting sense of disappointment that Isabella recognised the figure crouched down examining the horse's legs.

Andrew jumped from the carriage. 'What ails him, Joseph?'

'I can't tell precisely,' Joseph said, 'but he refuses to take another step.'

Andrew ran his hand down each leg in turn, from withers to feathered fetlock. 'I can feel nothing amiss.'

'Here. A muscle strained, or ruptured.' Joseph guided Andrew's fingers to the spot. The horse shuddered and tossed its huge head. 'I tried to get him to go a little further but he won't be coaxed. And the other can't pull the weight alone. We need a fresh beast. Nothing less will do.'

Andrew knew of a farm not too far off so, leaving Margaret and the children in Samuel and Joseph's care, he went to enquire where they could borrow another animal.

Meanwhile, Isaac led the lame horse to the back of the cart and tethered it securely. Isabella went with him and stood quietly stroking the carthorse's muzzle and reaching up to pat its shoulder. She had never been so close to such a large beast before, yet felt only the tiniest bit afraid, though she could feel the muscles bulge beneath the skin and knew what injuries its giant hooves could inflict. Isaac watched her with approval and admiration, but did not say as much, being unsure how his words would be received.

A short while after Andrew's departure, a carriage approached from the direction of Sedbergh, drew alongside Joseph's cart and came to a halt. A man of stocky build, wearing a coat of rough cloth, climbed out and nodded to Joseph with whom he was clearly acquainted, then enquired of Margaret whether he could be of assistance. Not wishing to be too familiar with a stranger, Margaret informed him, rather stiffly, that her husband, Mr Paitson, had gone for help.

'Forgive me,' the man said, removing his hat. 'I omitted to introduce myself. Roger Moser, joiner, of Stricklandgate, Kirkby Kendal. And this is George, my son.' Roger indicated a young boy, of similar build to his own, still seated in the carriage.

Margaret, now smiling, extended her hand. 'Then we'll soon be neighbours! We're on our way to a house on the same street.'

Roger Moser expressed his pleasure at the prospect and assured Margaret that his wife would be pleased to help them settle into their new residence in any way she could. In fact, when he reached home he would immediately instruct Elizabeth to prepare victuals against the Paitson family's arrival, if Margaret would tell him how many mouths they were.

Young George left them to their conversation and wandered round to the back of the cart where he was surprised to see a girl no older than himself, standing unperturbed beside a carthorse of huge dimensions.

Isaac nodded to the newcomer. 'George.'

George returned the nod. 'Isaac.'

'And I'm Isabella! Are you two friends?' Isabella looked with interest from one to the other. George admired her direct manner, free from the coyness he had come to associate with girls.

'My house is on the same street as yours,' he said quickly, before Isaac could speak.

'Then we'll see each other often!' Isabella was delighted to have acquired two friends before she had even reached the town. 'And where is your house, Isaac?'

'He lives in Kirkland,' George interposed again. 'At the opposite end from your house and mine. My father says Kirkland is full of thieves and scoundrels who deserve to be whipped and placed in the stocks. And my mother says Kirkland folk don't care if their infants drown in the Well Syke.'

'There are plenty of good folk in Kirkland,' Isaac insisted.

Isabella was at a loss to know whom to believe. On balance she favoured Isaac's account as he actually lived there. She also thought it a little unkind of George to say such unpleasant things about Isaac's home, but that did not prevent her wanting George to be her friend; there was something exciting about him. You could have adventures with George, and Isabella liked the idea of adventures.

Just then, Sarah came round the corner of the cart, a half-eaten apple in one hand. Seeing Isabella in conversation with George, she hurried to join them. She wished to recommend herself to George by demonstrating she felt the same degree of compassion for the injured horse as Isabella did, so she held out the remains of her apple on her palm for a titbit. The horse's wet nose snuffled the offering and a frothy mass of saliva accumulated round its mouth as it chomped.

'Oh!' Sarah cried, as a portion of foam landed on her sleeve. 'How horrid. How revolting.' She withdrew her hand sharply.

Startled by the sudden movement, the carthorse snorted, tossed its head back showing the whites of its eyes and took a few nervous sideways steps. Frightened of being trampled, Sarah moved to one side but stumbled and fell to the ground. She stayed there, white faced and clutching her ankle while Isabella went quickly to squat at her side.

'Can you wriggle your toes?' Isabella asked. This was what Mamma asked William the time he fell out of the sycamore behind the farmhouse.

'I can, but it hurts me very badly.' Sarah spoke in a faint voice.

'Then it's not broken,' Isabella announced. 'It's only sprained and will swell up hugely.'

The children formed a circle and stared at the ankle for quite a while, waiting for it to puff up like a ball. When it failed to do so, Isabella tried unsuccessfully to pull Sarah to her feet. Sarah cast an appealing look in George's direction, her eyes glistening with green tears.

George hesitated: on one hand he was reluctant to leave Isabella and Isaac together in case they became close friends in his absence; on the other hand, he felt sure Isabella would be favourably impressed if he helped her sister.

'Here, take my hand,' he said at last. 'Only wait while I clean it.' He spat into his palms then rubbed his hands on his breeches.

Roger Moser, meanwhile, was beginning to regret his promise to Margaret; he had not reckoned the cost of purchasing provisions for so many mouths, but it was too late now to withdraw. He must reach home as soon as possible and tell his wife what he had done, but he could not leave without his son.

Coming round the end of the cart, Roger stopped to take in the scene; a girl was lying on the ground clearly in distress, Joseph's Thompson's son attended to the agitated horse, while George did nothing but polish his hands on his breeches!

'Good for nothing! Why don't you offer assistance to this unfortunate young woman?' Roger admonished, as he boxed his son's ears. George kept his eyes on the ground and made no attempt to explain himself, but Isabella saw how his cheeks burned at the humiliation. Ordering George to follow, Roger Moser gathered Sarah in his arms and delivered her to her mother's care.

'To answer your question,' said Isaac when he and Isabella were alone again, 'George is my friend but sometimes he pretends he's not.'

At last the weary travellers looked down on Kirkby Kendal, encircled by hills as though snuggled in the palm of a giant hand. From here the road dropped steeply towards the northern end of the town where a constant flow of horse-drawn vehicles and pedestrians crossed the River Kent by means of a bridge.

Line upon line of tenters could be seen crisscrossing the land beside the river and stretching out over the fells above the town; Isabella thought the frames resembled rows of infantrymen with raised bayonets threatening to tighten their siege of Kirkby Kendal and slaughter the inhabitants.

As their carriage proceeded slowly up Stramongate, the Paitson children fell silent, overwhelmed by the confusion of houses on either side. Children playing before the doorways left their games to stare; Margaret instructed her family to pay no heed to the rudeness, but Agnes disobeyed and stuck out her tongue.

To Isabella the houses seemed to jostle for position as might happen in a crowd; some leaned forward till they almost toppled into the street or stood on tiptoe to get a better look, others peeked out shyly from the shadows, or curtseyed with heads bowed. At intervals little openings punctuated the line of buildings and, peeping through, Isabella caught glimpses of half-hidden garths behind the main street; little worlds set apart, where the less well-to-do lived and laboured in cottages with outside staircases, huddled round a courtyard.

'Welcome to you, Andrew.' A man in a coat of coarse cogware stepped close to the carriage. 'I heard you were coming back. May you and your family find happiness here.'

'I believe we shall.' Andrew looked at Margaret whose face was all smiles.

The air was clotted with the smell of burning peat and tallow candles, the yeasty odour of dowk-houses and fulling stocks and the foul stench of tanpits. Freshly-butchered carcasses hung in the street which was awash with gore and guts.

They came to the Fish Market which sold upwards of thirty varieties, most of them unfamiliar. Isabella, who never could abide the smell of fish, pinched her nose and Margaret slid her hand into the pocket which hung at her waist and withdrew her scent bottle and sprinkled a few drops on Isabella's sleeve.

'Look, Mamma!' Nancy exclaimed. 'Did you ever see such a beautiful gown?'

'I'll stitch you one just like it, my dear.' Margaret was discomfited to note that, compared with the style of garments worn by the respectable folk of Kirkby Kendal, her family's clothes were outmoded.

The carriage turned into the main street and drove on past Market Place where stalls were piled high with all manner of produce, and on past open-fronted shops selling anything you could wish to buy. At last they came to a halt near the bottom of Stricklandgate.

Men and women left their work and stood in their doorways or stepped into the street to greet the newcomers. Margaret fell easily into conversation and Andrew watched with pleasure as she moved amongst them with a grace he had not seen her exhibit for many years.

Keys were inserted in locks and the front door opened to reveal a wood-panelled interior which the children entered, their footsteps echoing in the emptiness. Isabella stood on tiptoe to put her eye to the little glass-covered hole at the side of the front door.

'Lift me up,' Agnes wailed. 'I want to see too.'

Meg strove to pick up the massive chain attached to the door and, having failed, called her sisters for help but even with their combined strength it was too heavy to lift.

'Each link is as thick as my arm!' Isabella exclaimed and wondered if that meant the thieves and burglars of Kirkby Kendal were especially strong.

They stepped down to the kitchen with its lingering odour of food cooked and consumed by another family, and shelves stained red and brown from spillages. They raced upstairs, running their fingers along the balustrade as they went. Isabella looked out of the upstairs window into the faces of the houses opposite, and wondered whether eyes peered back at her from behind each curtain.

'Let's see what's outside,' Nancy said. 'I noticed a door leading out through the back kitchen.'

They trooped down again and stood in the long garden. The odour of evening meals being cooked in the houses ranged on either side of theirs, reached their noses, and they heard the clink of cooking pots. A woman called to her child, a man swore an oath and something crashed to the floor. To Isabella it seemed the residents of Kirkby Kendal were packed so close they had no room to breathe.

A cone-shaped mound rose sharply to the back of the street and Isabella feared that if they did not behave themselves, the hill would topple and crush their house as punishment. Even after she had gone back inside, she could not shake off the feeling it was observing everything she did.

Elizabeth Moser brought them food as her husband

promised, rounds of beef trapped between two chunks of bread, and in return Margaret gave Elizabeth a jar of damson jelly. Isabella went to the door with her mother and watched Elizabeth walk back in the direction of Market Place then disappear into an archway. So that was where George lived!

When their stomachs were full, Nancy shepherded the children upstairs to bed but they took a long while to fall asleep on account of the noises from without.

Alone at last, Margaret took stock of their new residence. She would have preferred it to be a little more commodious, not quite as tightly squeezed by houses on either side, and situated a little further from the Workhouse. However, she would make the best of it, and was already wondering which walls to hang with wallpaper and which to paint and what colours would best suit. Margaret wondered also whether it was better to hold a tea party of her own or wait for her neighbours to make the first move.

An excess of wondering left her agitated and to calm herself, she opened her mahogany box and took out a little bible. The pages fell open at a section towards the end. Margaret turned to her favourite psalm.

Thou hast my table richly deck'd, in despite of my foe:
Thou hast my head with balm refresh'd, my cup doth
overflow.
And finally while breath doth last, thy grace shall me
defend;
And in the house of God will I my life forever spend.

Samuel lay on the truckle bed in the front room, as it was too late to make the return journey to Dent, and listened while Andrew Paitson and Roger Moser debated the issues of the day over a flagon of fruit wine given by one of Andrew's suppliers.

'Tell me,' Roger said, 'what do you say to Fenwick's victory? Lowther's man was well and truly trounced, albeit Fenwick only entered the race at the eleventh hour.' He drank deep as though re-enacting the celebrations.

Andrew refilled their goblets. He suspected the outcome of the recent election would have been very different, had Lord Lowther stood as candidate himself; however, he thought it unwise to become embroiled in discussion of the topic, Kirkby Kendal being a Whig stronghold. Andrew counted himself a royalist, being an ardent supporter of the Bonnie Prince.

He was relieved when Roger turned the conversation towards his brothers who were enjoying a remarkable degree of prosperity as ironmongers in London. Andrew listened with interest, and on occasion with horror, to the description of life in the overcrowded capital, and was grateful he did not have to live there himself.

The flagon was nigh empty and both men were slouched, loose-limbed and pleasantly fuzzle-headed, in their chairs when Roger noticed how late it was. He thanked Andrew for a most agreeable evening and made his way to the front door, pausing for a moment at the foot of the staircase.

'Your daughters will grow up cheek by jowl with my son,' he said with a boldness born of drink. 'Who knows where that may lead?'

'I would have no objection,' Andrew chuckled. 'But I doubt I will have any say in the matter.'

Isabella, lying awake upstairs, overheard them and wondered what it was that Papa would not object to, and why Mr Moser found it so amusing. More importantly, she wondered how long it would be before she once more set eyes upon George and Isaac, her new friends.

CHAPTER 4

1771

Isabella had chosen a spot well to the south of Nether Bridge, where the river looped back upon itself as though relaxing after all the work required of it by the mills and tanneries. Here the three friends were out of sight of the town, busy waterfowl paddled among the reeds and in general the balance between man and nature was restored.

George and Isaac discarded their boots and waded into the river, gasping at its coldness and placing their feet gingerly on the riverbed. How Isabella longed to join them! Not for the first time, she wished she had been born a boy. Her mother allowed her to remove her shoes and stockings and dip her toes in the shallows, but forbade anything further as it would be improper for a girl.

And when Isabella asked why, Mamma told her that girls and women must accept their lot without question or protest, which was no answer at all. Isabella had witnessed Margaret's protests often enough but she thought it wiser not to mention this.

'Do you think it's safe?' she asked. 'The current's even stronger than when we were here before.' She referred to a time earlier that year when the river tore up graves in the churchyard and swept away Blind Beck Bridge.

'I'm not afraid,' said George, hoping to win Isabella's admiration. 'The current's strong, but I'm stronger.'

'We won't go far from the bank,' said Isaac, hoping to allay Isabella's fears. 'And we won't stay in the water too long.'

Turning to face each other the two boys flayed the surface with their arms, raising showers of sparkling spray and laughing in delight. Bracing themselves against the current's drag they moved closer and whipped up ever denser clouds of droplets until both were blinded.

George opened his mouth to call a truce; at precisely

the same moment Isaac whisked a fountain directly into his friend's face so that George could not avoid taking in a mouthful. He struggled to inhale but water blocked his airways and for a few terrifying moments he feared he would never draw another breath, then with indescribable relief he heard the hoarse whistle of air entering his chest.

'Are you trying to drown me?' George shouted, furious with Isaac for making a fool of him, and what was worse, in front of Isabella.

'Your mouth just happened to be open,' said Isaac. 'I didn't mean to harm you. Let's go back now.' He turned towards the bank.

'First we'll see how you like this!' George grabbed Isaac's arm and forced him down until his face touched the water.

Isaac was familiar with George's sudden outbursts of temper, though he could not fully understand them as he never experienced such strong emotions himself. Isaac simply accepted the episodes as an essential aspect of their friendship; and George was indeed a true and loyal friend. More than once, he had put his strength at Isaac's disposal when fisticuffs broke out in the yard behind the school or when Isaac rescued helpless puppies from their good-for-nothing tormentors.

Besides, Isaac knew that without George he would not be able to sustain his friendship with Isabella, and since he first saw her chasing hens in Dentdale, Isaac had wanted to be Isabella's friend. He recognised in her the same unalloyed metal which formed the core of his own character. But Isabella loved to ask questions and carry on debates which left him tongue-tied and perplexed; she would never be satisfied with his company without George to complete the triangle.

'Now you have shown me, let me go.' Isaac struggled to free himself. 'I have no wish to fight.'

'Because you're a coward!' cried George. 'You tried to

drown me but you won't fight hand to hand!' George attempted to kick Isaac's legs from under him.

George had the advantage in weight and strength, but Isaac put his faith in the adage "attack is the best defence." He began to kick George's shins and thighs, and with his free hand punch any bodily part he could reach. In reply, George wrapped his arms round Isaac's midriff and squeezed and squeezed until his prisoner gasped for breath.

By this time George was not only angry with Isaac, but also with his father for the habit of humiliating him in public, with his mother for scolding him every time his little sister cried and with his little sister for crying in the first instance. Sensing a renewed intensity, Isaac squirmed and twisted in earnest. When he was at last free, Isaac scrabbled onto George's back and rode him like a stallion, pressing his heels into George's flanks and applying an open-handed whip to his rump.

A pair of urchins stopped chasing rats in the nearby brake and stood and watched, then began to mimic the two combatants, shrieking with laughter as they did so. George's cheeks flushed and his eyes filled with tears.

'That's enough!' Isabella shouted. 'Come on, let's go to the Castle and play at being knights.' In respect of temper, Isabella occupied a position part way between George and Isaac, that is she felt anger burn within her, but never submitted to it entirely.

It took a number of attempts, but eventually Isabella persuaded George and Isaac to end the skirmish, and they set off side by side towards the bank. They had not gone far when George stuck his foot out so that Isaac tripped; then George pushed hard against Isaac's shoulder, sending him sideways into the water. George gave a series of triumphant whoops and awarded himself a round of applause, much to the delight of the urchins who echoed his jubilation.

'That was unfair!' cried Isabella indignant at George's deceitful behaviour. 'Isaac thought you'd done fighting. I thought so too. Where is he, Georgie? I can't see him.'

Trusting her mother would suspend the rules in cases of necessity, Isabella knotted the hem of her gown around her waist and stepped into the river. Supposing Isaac were to drown, how could she bear to tell his parents? George, now fighting back tears of remorse, returned to the spot where Isaac fell and, with Isabella's assistance, lifted the limp body above the water and carried it ashore.

Isaac's face was the colour of the grass on which they laid him. They discussed how best to drain the water from his chest but, before they could begin, Isaac succumbed to a fit of coughing so violent they were afraid he would spew forth his innards.

'Don't worry.' Isaac opened his eyes and sat up. 'I'm not drowned!' His voice was like the croak of a frog.

'I'm glad to hear it!' Isabella smiled. 'For a while I was afraid you might be.'

They stretched out side by side, drying in the sun like lengths of cloth on tenter frames. The grass prickled their backs and insects crawled over their limbs. Isabella caught a beetle and held it in her palm admiring its glossy greenness, but it tried frantically to climb out of the hollow so she put it on the grass and watched it scuttle away.

Seeing the fun was over, the urchins turned their attention to a mangy rat trapped in a jar, and debated whether to keep it as a pet or eat it, and if the latter whether or not its taste would be improved by broiling.

'Mark my words young man,' Isabella wagged her finger at George and mimicked the voice of Elizabeth Moser, 'that temper will be the ruin of you.'

'It comes from somewhere outside,' said George miserably, 'and it won't let go. It gives me a jolt as if someone has kicked me, or hit me with a stout stick. I wish it would stop.'

Isaac examined a cut on his knee; his father Joseph would have advised licking it, in the way animals lick their wounds, but Isaac was reluctant to do that in front of his friends. Isabella carried out an inspection of the injury and recommended Isaac show it to the apothecary. George offered to tear off a piece of his shirt to serve as a bandage. Isaac hated being fussed over and insisted his knee would wait while he got home.

Isabella squinted at the sun and thought how blessed she was. Since coming to Kirkby Kendal she had formed friendships with her fellow pupils, though they were only whispering friends because Miss Selby was very strict; with their neighbours in Stricklandgate, like Martha in the house next door; and with the families Isabella played with after church on Sundays who dared one another to reach out a hand to touch the garish serpents and dragons which slithered and hissed in a giant frieze across the walls. But of all her friends she liked George and Isaac the best.

Mamma thought it unseemly for her to go about in the company of boys but Papa said it could do no harm since Isabella's chest was still as flat as the table top. This implied Isabella's chest would not stay flat forever, and she approached Alice one day, when she was scouring the skillet in the back yard, and asked her to illuminate. Alice thought carefully before giving her reply, and having given it, refused to say more.

'You know those two spots upon your chest, Miss Bella? Well, they're not pimples. So when they itch and begin to swell, don't go picking at them.' Which answer enlightened Isabella not one jot.

'What do you think?' Isabella asked. 'Will we stay friends for ever and ever?'

'I expect we will,' said Isaac, never having given the matter any thought.

'Not if they send me to London,' George said

gloomily.

He introduced the notion of being sent to London to join his uncles into most conversations, either as a means of impressing his friends or to gain their sympathy. Roger Moser used the prospect as a means of disciplining his son, either in the guise of a reward i.e. the chance to make a fortune in the capital, or a punishment i.e. exiled from everything that was familiar. Everyone knew George's parents would never, in reality, send their only son so far from home.

'Let's promise to stay friends.' Isabella pulled up her knees and wrapped her arms around them. 'Even when we get old. We should do something for a sign, so we'll never forget.'

Isaac suggested they each make the promise then shake hands, all six hands at the same time, but the others thought this too bland. George proposed cutting their wrists, mingling their blood then each drinking a few drops; he mimed the cutting and mingling and drinking with such verisimilitude that it was Isabella's complexion which now reflected the colour of grass.

Her own notion was to take a lock of hair from each of their heads, then work the locks together in the form of a plait as a symbol of unity, an idea which gained only lukewarm approval from the boys but was finally agreed upon as the least bad proposal. The three friends set off to find a sharp instrument with which to cut off the locks, a knife or a pair of scissors.

They crossed Nether Bridge in the wake of an unusual figure, swathed in a long brown robe and muttering to himself as he shuffled forward. They had all heard of the Anchorite hermits who lived in the fields behind Kirkbarrow and had seen their servants in the town. Mothers frightened their children into obedience with stories of being locked up in a hermit's cell if they misbehaved. Alice once sprinkled water from the

Anchorite Well on the pustules which broke out all over her sister's baby; a few days later the infant's skin was completely free of sores.

George began to mimic the man's progress, exaggerating the shuffling and babbling until they became grotesque. Passers-by turned to watch with amusement and a few idle louts fell in behind. Enjoying the audience, George increased his antics and was rewarded with appreciative laughter. Isabella was horrified. The poor man had done nothing to warrant being ridiculed in this manner.

'I'm ashamed to be seen with you, Georgie,' she whispered. 'I'll go home if you don't leave off right now.' George bowed to his audience and resumed his normal gait.

'It was only a little fun,' he said, somewhat shamefaced. 'I won't do it any more, I promise.'

A team of pack-horses clattered by, their hooves skittering over the cobbles and their panniers full of coarse cloth on its way south. Partially obscured by the animals, the Anchorite servant disappeared into the narrow opening of Kirkbarrow Lane.

The children hurried to catch up but, when they entered the lane, the robed figure was nowhere to be seen. As they turned back towards the main street, he appeared suddenly from nowhere and blocked their way. His hood was folded back to reveal a heavily lined face and stern eye.

'Have you nothing better to do? Why mock an old man going quietly about his business?' His gaze settled on Isabella. 'And you my daughter, why do you throw in your lot with these scoundrels?'

Isabella felt her cheeks flame.

'My friend here has a cut,' said George, hastily stepping forward and pointing to Isaac. 'It's deep and very painful. We're going to bathe it in water from your holy well.'

Isaac duly displayed his knee and groaned. The Anchorite servant hesitated for a moment, eyes flitting between the two, then broke into a rich chuckle and slapped George on the back.

'You'll go a long way, my son, with wits as fleet as that!' He turned his attention to Isaac's knee. 'The cut is deep but neat. It'll heal well enough if smeared with balm of honey and knight's milfoil. I know where I can find a jar.'

Isaac thanked him kindly but insisted his father would apply one of the treatments kept in the stables for use on the horses. Everyone laughed.

'Can I ask you a question?' Isabella was determined not to lose this opportunity.

'I have time to answer one question.' The Anchorite servant gave Isabella an encouraging smile.

'What do the hermits wear? And what do they eat and are they allowed to have friends?'

'I protest! That was three questions in the guise of one. Let me see; they wear garments of the coarsest cloth for they've chosen absolute simplicity, they eat whatever the townspeople leave at our door, and as to friends, no, they have no need of human company. Now I must attend to the carpenters.'

He moved off with the same shuffling gait, and accompanied by the same continuous muttering as if this was an essential component of his progress. Half way down the lane he waved but did not turn round.

Isabella felt the disapproving eye of Kendal Fell upon her as she drew near her house. She crept in through the back door so that her mother would not notice her wet underskirt and stockings. Alice was in the kitchen and supplied a length of cloth to dry Isabella's feet and fetched a fresh pair of stockings and promised not to tell, but as Isabella was crossing the hall, she met her mother who demanded to know why she had used the back door.

'I've told you many times, Bella. Only the servants come through the kitchen. Daughters of the house should enter directly by the front door.'

Isabella, who hated to tell a lie, admitted she wished to conceal the fact she had paddled in the river. Margaret was surprised by this confession for, as a rule, Isabella could be relied upon not to disobey orders. In spite of her mother's questioning, Isabella gave no fuller explanation, lest George's father punish him for his attack upon Isaac.

Sitting up in bed, Isabella examined the three locks of hair cut off with a pair of scissors supplied by Isaac's mother. Her own hair was dark and curly, the other two were of lighter shades and, moreover, straight and limp with no will of their own. She tried to work the strands into a single braid but found, to her disappointment, they were too short. Instead, she secured them with a ribband then tucked them under her side of the mattress.

'You can't stay friends with George and Isaac all your life,' Sarah warned. 'When you're married your husband won't allow it.' She climbed into bed and pulled the covers towards her, leaving Isabella's arm and leg exposed to the cold.

'Then I won't marry.' Isabella slowly pulled the covers back until she had sufficient to keep herself warm. 'At least not until I find a husband who will allow it.'

'It would be hard to find such a husband,' said Sarah. 'And even if you did, do you imagine the women George and Isaac marry will allow them to continue their friendship with you?'

It had never occurred to Isabella that George and Isaac might one day take wives. At first the notion displeased her, but on reflection she decided their wives could cut strands from their hair and join the pact.

'Once you marry,' Nancy declared, with all the wisdom of her nineteen years, 'you won't enjoy the company of other men. Your husband will demand your full attention and fulfil all your needs.' Nancy was soon to marry her sweetheart, John Jackson, and take up residence with him in his home town of Bolton.

'Stop talking about husbands,' Agnes whined. 'Tell me a story else I shall scream.'

Isabella lay awake wondering what the Anchorite servant was actually saying when he muttered and whether she ought to choose absolute simplicity and, if so, would she have to give up tying her hair with ribbands.

Isaac could not sleep due to the pain in his knee so he devoted his time to praying that George would not be punished for causing the injury nor Isabella for going into the water when she was forbidden.

George was too troubled by the thought of what his father would do if word reached him regarding the circumstances in which Isaac acquired his cut knee, to sleep. To distract himself, he composed the following list of reasons why he liked Isabella:

i   She knew more than he did but never boasted.
ii Her clear eyes looked at him directly, without veil, and always with kindness.
iii She could be serious if the occasion warranted but her smile was never far away.
iv Her hair curled and twisted no matter how she tried to smooth it.

At the other end of town, the Anchorite servant knelt on the stone floor and prayed for the children who followed him across Nether Bridge earlier that day. The plump one was too full of himself but had a generous heart and meant no harm; with guidance he would thrive. The girl had more brains than were good for her, but she had heart in equal measure, he was sure of that; she would one day make an exemplary wife and mother. And the lean one? Ah, the lean one would go quietly through life making no fuss and bearing no grudges. He was the one the Anchorite servant would choose for a son.

CHAPTER 5

2007

'Family History classes?' The librarian consulted her screen. 'What level are you looking for?' She pushed her glasses up into her hair and waited impatiently for Tibby's answer.

'What levels do you have?'

'Beginners and Advanced.' The woman handed Tibby a course information sheet. 'We're not running Intermediate this year. Term starts next month and you can enrol on the night. There's no fee for pensioners.' She looked at Tibby doubtfully. 'You'll need basic IT skills, even for the Beginners class.'

'That won't be a problem.' Tibby managed a smile.

Did she really look like someone who'd never used a computer? Perhaps she shouldn't have stopped colouring her hair. People dismissed you when you went grey, unless it was that stunning silver.

When she got home Tibby checked the price of John Field bibles. Just out of curiosity, she wasn't going to sell. There were no exact matches, but some of the listed editions were very similar to Isabella's. They weren't worth a lot, in fact the market for old bibles was pretty much saturated. Of course Isabella's would be more valuable if it had provenance, which it might do if Tibby could trace Isabella and Peter and their families.

The site directed her to an article on bible printing in the 1600s. Apparently many contained errors. Serious ones like, "Thou shalt commit adultery"! John Field's mistakes included "Know ye not that the unrighteous shall inherit the kingdom of God?" Even then the scoundrel managed to get himself appointed official publisher to Oliver Cromwell!

The secondary school where the evening classes were

held was mostly glass and concrete, the corridors were endless, the walls were bare and the whole building felt bleak and uncared for. Tibby remembered her own secondary school as a friendly and colourful place, but then it was much smaller. People were wandering about holding leaflets and looking puzzled. She wandered with them for a while then discovered the Reception desk.

'Family History? In the senior library.' The man behind the desk gave her directions.

'I haven't enrolled yet.' Tibby held out the form, duly completed.

'The course tutor does that. You'll be all right. Pensioners don't pay.' He looked at her as though he was personally responsible for subsidising her fee and she should be grateful.

The library, when she finally reached it, was an improvement on the rest of the building. The walls were covered in posters and poems and book reviews and the different sections were colour coded. Tibby scanned the bookshelves but didn't recognise any of the titles.

There were twelve of them in the class, ranging in age from twenty (on behalf of her grandmother) to eighty (on the instructions of his wife). The more dedicated came armed with plastic files and ring binder folders, A4 pads and acid-free wallets for preserving old photos and documents. One man brought a dictaphone in case he couldn't write fast enough. Tibby felt unprepared by comparison.

While the course tutor was busy with the frustrating intricacies of enrolment, they introduced themselves. It turned out the others were all tracing members of their own families, most of them local. They sat in silence while Tibby showed them the little bible and explained she wanted to trace Isabella and Peter. They didn't actually say so but she was pretty sure they thought she was wasting her time. It made her feel like an outsider and she wondered if she'd done the right thing by joining the class. Well, there was no need to come back next week if she didn't like it.

The tutor introduced himself as Jez and boasted he'd spent over twenty years building his own family tree which to date consisted of over two thousand individuals, then regaled them with anecdotes illustrating the triumphs and failures he'd met with during the course of his search.

He was in his early fifties and scruffily dressed. A natural performer, but to Tibby he sounded stale, as if he'd covered the same material a hundred times before, which he probably had.

'You need perseverance and determination,' he told them, 'and you must be well organised. But the biggest factor by far is luck.' They all laughed. 'No, I mean it. I can't remember how often it's happened. I'm completely stuck then something turns up quite by chance, and I get a breakthrough.'

He described the origins and types of surname, and outlined the early history of parish records, illustrating what he said with fuzzy slides. Two members of the class chatted continuously while he was talking. One man nodded off and began to snore.

Afterwards Jez passed round a list of Latin terms used in genealogy and a list of common abbreviations for first names, which was interesting. Tibby hadn't realised Nancy was an informal version of Anne, and Sally of Sarah.

'That's a coincidence!' A woman with a face as smooth and creamy as a new potato addressed Tibby. 'You're looking for someone called Isabella, aren't you? It says here Tibby's short for Isabella. Did you know that? Sorry. Silly thing to say. Of course you know. Sorry.'

'It's okay,' Tibby smiled. 'My mother chose my name but my grandmother didn't think I looked like an Isabella. She called me Tibby and it stuck.'

After the break, Jez gave them each a password for the

computers and showed them how to access online records of births, deaths and marriages without subscribing. Someone asked about the National Archives at Kew. Jez told him that was scheduled for another week. Best not move forward too rapidly. Tibby volunteered to help a rather large gentleman covered in tattoos who confessed to being a computer novice.

It was fun exploring unfamiliar sites and learning the jargon and it was good to be with people again. She'd been a bit of a hermit since retiring. She was glad she'd come. Before they left, Jez handed out five-generation ancestral charts plus continuation sheets.

'They probably look a bit daunting to you right now,' he said, 'but you'll be surprised how quickly you fill them in.'

Tibby took one set for the Paitsons and one set for the Mosers.

As she drove home she wondered what the others would say if she told them she knew nothing about her own father. Tibby's mother never mentioned him; as far as she was concerned he didn't exist. No doubt she wanted to keep a low profile. You heard of single women forced to give up their babies for adoption or shut up in an asylum for immoral behaviour in those days. Presumably in Isabella's time it was even worse, at least it was if you came from a respectable family. Nowadays of course there were no rules. All very well for the adults but not so good for the children.

Anyway neither Tibby's mother nor grandparents ever talked about her father and Tibby hadn't asked. What words would you use to talk about someone who existed only in your imagination? Not that she thought much about her father when she was growing up. She might have if she'd been unhappy, but she wasn't. Her mother did her best to treat her two daughters equally, as did Tibby's stepfather.

Tibby sensed of course that he loved Lottie, his own daughter, best but he didn't show it, not in concrete ways at least. If he bought Lottie sweets then Tibby got some too, in spite of rationing, and if he took Lottie to the pictures Tibby went along with them. Mostly she let people think he was her real father, and if this didn't satisfy them, then she claimed her father died in the war. That usually shut them up.

When the Sunday School teacher noticed her surname wasn't the same as Lottie's and asked if her real father was dead, Tibby told him she didn't have a real father so he couldn't be dead.

'Everyone has a father,' the teacher said, resting an irritating hand on the top of her head. 'You have one too, even if you've never seen him.'

'Then God must be my real father. I've never seen him.'

He made Tibby stand in the corner for being disrespectful. Her cheeks burned so hot she thought her eyes would turn into coddled eggs. Since hearing stories about cannibals eating missionaries she'd been terrified of being cooked alive. Even now she kicked her hot water bottle to the bottom of the bed in case her liver and kidney overheated while she slept.

It was a couple of days before Tibby had time to take out Jez's guide to online resources and start her quest for Isabella. She brought up the page for searching births, deaths and marriages. It asked for a beginning and an end date.

She didn't know Isabella's date of birth but it couldn't be later than 1774 and it was unlikely to be before 1727 in view of the fact she was still around in 1827 when she gave the bible to Peter. Tibby entered the values and pressed Go. "No matches" appeared on the screen. She repeated the process in case she'd made a mistake. Nothing.

Okay, how about Isabella Paitson marriages? Three candidates! Excellent. Tibby looked at them one by one. Damn! They were all born later than 1774, which ruled them out. Disappointing so far but the tutor had warned them the online records were incomplete. Right then, Isabella Paitson deaths. Tibby punched in the parameters. Again, "No matches". This was really disheartening.

'But she wasn't Paitson when she died, was she?' Lottie said when she phoned for an update. 'She was Isabella Thompson.'

'Of course! I can't believe I'm so stupid!' Tibby laughed. 'I don't know what's happened to my brain.'

That was another of Lottie's worries, that Tibby's brain would quickly decay if she didn't keep using it. A search for Isabella Thompson deaths brought up thousands of results, far too many to check. If only Isabella hadn't married someone with such a common surname.

Over the next few days Tibby unearthed everything there was to know about the Paitsons, visiting different sites and exploring every angle. It was fun but also very frustrating. She kept discovering something interesting then going back for another look only to find it had disappeared. She soon disciplined herself to keep records.

The Paitsons were a conservative lot when it came to naming their offspring. Every family had at least one Andrew and one William, often two. Which seemed odd until Tibby realised that when one of their children died, the parents recycled the name.

She was shocked by the number of infant deaths. She came across one woman whose date of death was the same as her child's date of birth and assumed someone had made a mistake when they entered the data. When it happened again and again Tibby realised that, of course, the mothers had died in childbirth.

The earliest Paitsons owned breweries and other small businesses like a timber yard and sawmill and were often involved in legal disputes. They seemed to originate in Cumberland then subsequent generations gradually spread out into other parts of the country.

Cumberland? Tibby let go the mouse, reached under her desk and pulled out the crumpled wrapping paper which came with the book. As she thought, the parcel was sent by Mosers & Sons, Kendal. Right on the doorstep of Paitson territory. It was true, the wrapping paper belonged to a more recent period, but Moser & Sons could be direct descendants of early Mosers living in Kendal. With the Paitsons living so close there was every chance the two families were related. This was looking more hopeful.

CHAPTER 6

1774

With the advent of her monthly flowers, Isabella left the carefree years of childhood behind and was obliged to start behaving like a woman. Margaret insisted she always cover her hair with a bonnet, though Isabella preferred it to hang loose, and she was forbidden to go anywhere after dark unless accompanied by one of her own family.

Furthermore, she was not to carry heavy things or run races or play with her hoop or exert herself in any way, for Margaret believed to do so would tear a young woman's womb and leave her barren.

'If that's the case,' Isabella asked, 'how is it Alice's sister has so many children when she exerts herself all day taking in washing and fetching and carrying in other folks' houses?'

'Alice and her sister are not our kind of people,' her mother explained. 'Their constitutions are ordered differently from ours.' Andrew, overhearing, reprimanded his wife for peddling nonsense.

One evening, Margaret presented Isabella with the diminutive bible she herself so often consulted, as a gift to mark Isabella's entry into womanhood. Margaret urged her daughter to seek in the pages of the book the strength to resist the many temptations which would beset her now she was a young woman.

'Temptation to do what?' Isabella asked her sister Nancy.

'Learn from the dogs and pigeons,' Nancy replied. 'Haven't you noticed what they do, or do you go about with your eyes closed?' Which enlightened Isabella not one jot so she put the same question to Martha, who lived next door.

'Have you never felt a delicious tingle?' said Martha. 'I mean, when you stand close to a young man, close enough for him to touch you if he wanted to.' She formed her lips into a seductive pout and tilted her head coquettishly in imitation of the infamous Fanny Murray.

Isabella experimented and stood close enough to William to see each separate bristle on his chin, which was not an easy thing to do as William liked to keep his distance, but nothing happened. She raised the question with George and Isaac but they denied all knowledge of tingles, delicious or otherwise, and looked so uncomfortable Isabella wished she had not asked.

As they, too, left childhood behind, Isaac's and George's time was increasingly taken up with duties assigned them by their respective fathers; Isaac was charged with oversight of the horses and carriages when Joseph Thompson was away from home, and George was often obliged to mind Roger Moser's workroom and deal with queries from prospective customers.

But this did not mean Isabella was deprived of their company. Whenever she was not required to assist with domestic tasks, she would contrive to pass an hour or two with Isaac, helping him apply grease to the axles of the carts and wagons so that the wheels rotated smoothly, or watching him repaint the exterior of the carriages, or, best of all, following him to the stables where the horses reached out to rub their muzzles against his chest as he greeted them one by one.

'Will you join your father's business?' Isabella asked, holding out a handful of oats to her favourite mare. 'Or will you learn a different trade altogether?'

'This is what I know,' Isaac said, 'and what I enjoy. I'm content to stay here for as long as there is a demand for carriers.'

'There's many ways a man can earn a living. You might prefer some other trade. How can you tell if you never try?' Isabella admired Isaac's consistency but she sometimes wished he would display a little more spirit.

Isaac looked about him. The smell of straw and dung, the snorting and whinnying, the scraping of hooves and the feel of muscles, bunching and sliding, under warm skin, these were all part of him and always would be.

'You may think me dull but I can't help that,' he said a little sadly. 'I will not be false to my own heart.'

At other times Isabella would visit George in his father's workroom which smelt of freshly cut oak, and every flat surface was coated with fine oak sawdust. Roger kept the room in perfect order and George was required to do the same. Isabella soon learned the names of the tools and where each was kept.

Chisels sat in racks above the joinery bench, with brace, hammer and mallet. Planes were arranged on the shelf beside the planing bench, which ran along the wall furthest from the fire. Saws hung in a row from pegs high up close to the ceiling, while augers and gimlets slotted into holes bored in a wooden bracket a little lower down.

'When will you be allowed to make your own chairs and tables?' Isabella asked. She ran her fingers along a length of oak, planed and sanded smooth as satin.

'I don't intend to take up joinery,' George said. 'I'm not going to spend my days sawing and chiselling and breathing in sawdust and making plain furniture for common folk.'

'Then how will you earn your living?' Isabella lifted a saw from its hook and pretended to cut a piece of timber in two.

'Take care, Bella, the teeth are sharp.' George took the saw from Isabella's hand. 'I'd like to be a merchant and buy and sell goods.'

'And what does your father say to that?'

'I've not yet told him.' George made a gloomy face. 'I can't find the courage. He's proud of his craft and expects me to follow in his footsteps. He'll be disappointed and angry if I tell him I don't intend to become a joiner.'

'But you must tell him. It'll only make it more difficult if you delay.' Isabella threw a handful of sawdust in the air and watched it pass through the shafts of light from the window.

George followed Isabella's advice and spoke to his father that very evening.

'What's wrong with joinery?' Roger Moser said. 'You won't find a more reliable trade. Folk will always require chairs for sitting and beds for sleeping and cabinets for keeping things in.' He brushed wood shavings impatiently from his leather apron while he waited for George's reply.

'I don't have an aptitude for it,' George muttered. 'I prefer to try something else.' He shifted his weight awkwardly from one foot to the other. Although he had the physique of a man, his limbs were clumsy and would not always obey instructions.

Roger demanded to know whether that something else was ironmongery, and if so then George was welcome to pursue that line of work in London.

'No, sir, not iron,' said George hastily. 'Certainly not iron. I choose leather.'

George knew perfectly well what he really wished to say, and had rehearsed the speech with Isabella that very morning, but now his mouth would not form the words and instead spoke absurdly of leather.

'What's that?' Elizabeth appeared in the doorway, cradling a baby in her arms. 'You'd rather soil your hands with stinking hides than work with sweet smelling timber?' She beckoned to her daughter who was playing in the hearth. 'Come, child. I need you to rock your sister's cradle while I see to the laundry.' The little girl stood up, wiped her nose on the hem of her frock and obediently followed Elizabeth from the room.

'You heard your mother,' Roger said. 'She doesn't want you working with leather. I'll not have you going against her wishes.'

'Wool, then,' said George miserably, convinced his mother said nothing of the kind. 'Folk will always need clothes and bedding.'

'If you mean to be a weaver, then you must think again. I can't afford to buy you a pair of studdles.' Roger eased himself back in his chair and stretched his legs wide.

It was clear that, no matter what George came up with, his choices would be dismissed one after another until he was left with no option but to settle for joinery. Isabella was right, he had no other chance of achieving his ambition than to speak out boldly.

'To tell you the truth, sir,' George mumbled, 'I'd prefer to buy and sell commodities than make them myself.'

'Now we have it!' Roger said triumphantly. 'You refuse to dirty your own hands but seek to profit from the labour of hands such as these!'

Roger displayed the calluses on his palms and fingers and the deformed thumbnail, the consequence of many misdirected blows from the hammer. He commanded George to hold out his hands and when he saw how smooth they were in comparison, Roger was overwhelmed by a sudden tenderness and felt ashamed of his former belligerence. George was right; it was best to keep one's hands free of blemishes. If his son chose to earn a living buying and selling what others made, Roger would not stand in his way.

The next step was to find a merchant willing to take George as apprentice, preferably a generous individual who would not demand too high a fee. Roger immediately thought of his neighbour, Andrew Paitson, and approached him without delay.

It did not take Andrew long to consider the request before conceding; George would make an agreeable assistant, Andrew surmised, for the lad displayed the ardour and warmth which were sadly lacking in his own son, William. Besides, George was Bella's friend and Andrew was happy to honour that friendship. Details were negotiated, indenture documents drawn up and duly signed by all parties.

'You know what they say,' Roger joked as he and George made their way back from the attorney's. 'The apprentice ends up marrying his master's daughter! Which one would you have? Agnes is the best match for age but poor sight spoils her looks, Isabella is quick-witted and already your close friend, but Sarah is the pearl amongst the sisters when it comes to beauty. Only beware Paitson doesn't do as Laban did, and trick you into taking plain Meg for your Leah!'

In choosing to trade in wool, George was in good company; Kirkby Kendal was built on wool and the best part of the town's population, and of the surrounding villages, depended upon wool for their living. Hill farmers shepherded their flocks and sold their fleeces to wool merchants who weighed and graded the fleeces before sending them to be washed in vats of urine; woolcombers pulled the flocks into rovings with carding combs, heated on charcoal stoves; spinners sat on balconies and spun the wool onto quills and bobbins; spullars sorted the yarn for quality; clothiers distributed it to websters, women in the main, who sat all day at their looms weaving the yarn into cloth.

Drysalters extracted dye from rocket, weld and madder, and dyers used the extracts in their dye-houses; ashburners burned bracken in kilns on the slopes of Kentmere for the making of potash lye; bowkers added the lye to boiling vats to remove lanolin and soap; fullers and feltmakers compressed woollens to strengthen the fibres before the lengths of cloth were stretched on tenter frames to dry; shearman raised the nap with freizing bats composed of teasels then cropped it short with shears; whilters added hems and borders; mercers and drapers distributed the bolts of cloth. The work was arduous but for the skilled, hardworking and astute, there was money to be made in textiles.

Andrew took his responsibilities seriously and saw to it that George learned something new each day, and there was a great deal to learn.

'The wool of the Blackface and Herdwick is short and full of kemps but the wool of the Silverdale is long and soft,' George told Isabella. 'The twist is put into the yarn during spinning for worsteds but after spinning for woollens.'

'No!' said Isabella, laughing. 'It's the other way round.'

'Kersey is double twilled,' George told his little sister. 'Linsey has a linen warp and woolsey a cotton one.' She listened attentively then repeated the words to the wooden doll in her lap.

George went from house to house with the badgers in Andrew's employ; whole families, from young children to the very old, watched pale and anxious as the badgers counted the harvest of their crooked knitting pins. He travelled out to hill farms in the autumn when yeomen rubbed a mixture of tar and rancid butter into the sheep's woolly coat, and he returned in the spring to help weigh the shorn fleeces and stitch them into wool packs.

For her part, Isabella was delighted with George's apprenticeship as it meant he was often at her house; he came first thing in the day to take instruction and again in the evenings to report to Andrew and plan for the morrow. Isabella, who, unlike her sisters, always took a keen interest in her father's business, joined them as often as she could. She sat at one end of the sofa beneath the window while George occupied the other end.

William rarely attended; George did not seek to

supplant William in Andrew's affections but was not averse to profiting by his absence, in terms of access to Isabella's company as well as in terms of financial reward.

Andrew's custom was to first settle the pressing questions, then introduce a series of topical issues to test George and Isabella's powers of discernment, such as whether he should deal only in coarse worsted hose or also in gentlemen's silk stockings and whether the principal five dyeing houses in Kirkby Kendal were right to form a price-fixing consortium.

Isabella and George came at the problems in different ways; she quickly formed opinions and was eloquent in expressing them, while he was slower to make up his mind but when he did, voiced his argument with more conviction. Watching the two of them, Andrew thought what an excellent husband George would make Isabella and what an asset she would be to him as a wife.

When they were done, Margaret fed George a slice of pan pudding or a dish of buttermilk sweetened with honey. Then Isabella saw him to the door and bade him goodnight under the watchful eye of Kendal Fell, which seemed nowadays to protect rather than threaten.

As he made his way home, George thought how much he liked the curve of Isabella's cheek when she smiled, and the brightness of her eyes, and the way she flapped and fluttered her hands when she spoke, and he recalled his father's words concerning the apprentice marrying his master's daughter.

It was all very well for George and Isaac, they were occupied with woollens and worsteds and horses and carriages, but how was Isabella to fill her days now that she had passed on from Miss Selby's Dame school? Isabella sometimes accompanied her mother to tea parties, but not too often because she found the conversation dull, and from time to time her mother sent her to distribute oatmeal and turnips to those who were in need. Her sisters were content with their stitching and shell work and knotting and flower drawing but for Isabella these things were not enough.

'There are books aplenty in the book case,' Andrew said, observing Isabella's restlessness, 'and more on the shelf in the back room.'

'I've read every one twice over!' Isabella declared.

She begged him to approach the gentleman who was guardian of Sandes Hospital for Widows, and also schoolmaster of Blue Coat School for the Children of the Poor, which was situated in the same yard, and arrange for her to become a regular visitor. Her father did what she asked and Isabella went daily to the Hospital and sat with the widows while they related the various harrowing circumstances which led to their destitution, never ceasing their spinning and weaving as they spoke. They looked forward to Isabella's visits because she displayed a genuine interest, never mind how often they repeated their stories, and because she ran errands for them when they asked.

Isabella liked listening to the widows, but not as much as she liked going into the classroom where she assisted with the small number of female pupils who attended the school. At first, Isabella was dismayed to see how little interest they displayed in their schoolwork compared with the great deal of interest they displayed in playing marbles, poking and pinching till their neighbour squealed, and consuming large quantities of beef and potato at midday. But Isabella devised ways of attracting and retaining their attention and was rewarded when they remembered what she taught, and even more so when they asked questions of their own devising.

One afternoon, after dismissing her pupils, Isabella went in search of the schoolmaster and found him instructing two boys, who sought admission in the Free

School, in the declination of Latin nouns. He looked up as Isabella appeared in the doorway.

'Yes Miss Paitson? Do you wish to consult me on some matter?' He would have called her Isabella, had they been alone, but addressed her more formally so as to preserve her authority in front of the pupils.

'Forgive me for disturbing your lesson, sir, but I wondered if I might spend some time in the library. I've read every book on my father's bookshelves and want something new.'

'Certainly you may!' The schoolmaster was delighted to find someone interested in furthering her knowledge. 'I'll unlock the room presently and you may stay as long as you wish. The books are not be removed from the premises, you understand. Indeed many are chained to the shelf.'

Isabella was overawed when she entered the library. One whole chamber dedicated to reading! The light was poor and the air stale, but Isabella did not care, indeed she thought the stuffiness and gloom rendered the atmosphere more scholarly. She went over to inspect the books arrayed on the shelves and was surprised to find a thick layer of dust coating each volume, indicating they had not been disturbed for many months.

She blew the dirt off the largest volume and read a few pages; the subject matter was ecclesiastical history and Isabella found it dull and dreary. She tried another, this time a book devoted to theological dispute, and found it no more appealing than the first.

There must be something here of interest. She explored the other shelves, and was heartened to discover a volume of works by Galen; she had heard of Galen's anatomical dissections and eagerly flicked away the broken cobwebs and husks of dead spiders, but when she opened the book she could understand nothing as the text was in Latin.

At last Isabella found a slim volume, at the end of one shelf, the cover of which was free from dust and cobwebs, suggesting it was popular with the pupils. She turned to the first page, fully prepared for another disappointment, and was pleased to discover the book was an English rendering of Torquato Tasso's *Gerusalemme Liberata*, an epic tale based on the first Crusade but embellished and augmented with stories of courageous knights and passionate love. Isabella began reading and was immediately transported to an exotic, unfamiliar world.

She put on wings of silver, fringed with gold, nimble and swift and, parting the winds and clouds, flew with Godfredo over the sea and earth to the land of Libanon where warriors from many nations were assembled, bold and brave and glistening in their steel armour. She followed Prince Tancredi into the forest to rest amongst the wild herbs under the greenwood shade and spied the pagan damsel who spread her hair to catch sweet breath from the cooling air.

She admired the warrior Clorinda, a savage tigress who scorned the arts used by silly women, and she wept when Armida and her lover joined hands, embraced and kissed, "together fainted and together died." And when the tyrant's men plucked off the beautiful Sophrina's veil and mantle and bound her tender, naked body, Isabella felt her cheeks redden with sensations she had not previously experienced.

'Have you found something to your taste?' The schoolmaster appeared suddenly at her side.

'I've finished for today.' Isabella closed the volume hurriedly. 'Thank you, and please may I use the library again?'

Isabella walked home in a dreamlike state. Now she understood why Sarah contrived to place herself at the end of the line of Paitsons in the pew on Sundays, with her body pressed against the boy who contrived to sit at the end of the line of Cockrofts; and why the Hodgon lad hanged himself in his father's warehouse when the girl he loved ran off with his closest friend. Although at present no one incited these sensations in Isabella, she anticipated the day when somebody would.

CHAPTER 7

1777

Isabella was not surprised when William announced he intended to remove to Bolton to set up independently. She thought it a wise decision, for there seemed little prospect of any improvement in his relations with Papa.

William chose his time wisely for, due to the outbreak of war in the Americas, the War Office was engaged in procurement of vast quantities of hose for the military and paid a good price for what it purchased. Although he was never much in evidence, Isabella would miss William, as she missed the wickerwork chair in the hall though she rarely sat in it.

On her way upstairs with a pile of newly laundered bed linen, Isabella encountered her father hovering in the hallway. He hoped to say his farewell to William in the house, not wishing others to witness the coldness his son displayed towards him, but William had not put in an appearance.

'What time did you arrange to meet?' enquired Isabella.

'He agreed not to go out without speaking with me,' Andrew said. 'He knows full well I've an engagement with Capstick at nine.'

He pulled on his gloves only to tug them off again. He checked his watch against the clock which stood in the corner of the hallway then pushed open the heavy front door and stepped into the street. Cattle were tethered as far as the eye could see and the air was filled with the sound of lowing, of farmers shouting at their stock and of the laughter of country folk come from all around for the Cattle Fair. But there was no sign of William.

Margaret came out of the kitchen where she was supervising the preparation of food for the travellers to consume in advance of the journey, and of a parcel of victuals to nourish them for the duration of it.

'William has never been good at timekeeping.' Margaret wiped the sweat from her face with the end of her fichu. 'Allow him a few minutes more.'

'I don't have a few minutes.' Andrew took his walking stick and tapped it on the floor in a restless and uneven rhythm. 'Kindly tell him I waited but, as he did not appear, I will see him off at the Commercial with the rest of you.' So saying, he set off down the street. Isabella and her mother exchanged looks of regret; why could William not make an effort on this important day?

Margaret returned to the kitchen and Isabella proceeded on her way upstairs to the room where Nancy, who was to escort William on his journey to Bolton, was attending to the packing of his trunk. Agnes came in Isabella's wake, bearing William's best frock-coat.

'Lay the bed linen directly on the bottom would you, Bella?' Nancy said. 'And you can leave that on the bed, Aggie. It should go in last else it'll be spoiled by creasing.' She surveyed the meagre collection of well-worn shirts and waistcoats laid out on her parents' four-poster. 'Is this really all the clothing William owns?'

'William would wear his shirts until they were threadbare,' Isabella said, 'if Mamma didn't insist he visit the tailor to be measured for new.'

'I'll have to order cambric and Holland and stitch some shirts myself,' Nancy declared. 'The quality and condition of a man's linen can determine his chances of success, as John Jackson, my good husband, is fond of saying.'

Drawn by the sounds of a commotion, the three sisters hurried over to the window. A fight between two dogs was underway on the street below, watched by a small gathering, some of whom were enjoying the spectacle while others were attempting to intervene. Nancy's soft bosom pressed against Isabella's shoulders as she leaned forward, straining to see.

Nancy was two years married but Isabella could not imagine her being passionate with her husband because John Jackson was bald headed and corpulent and never laughed. This must account for the absence of babies, Isabella decided.

At last one brave young man dragged the bloodied animals apart, just in time to prevent one from tearing the throat of the other. While Nancy and Isabella resumed packing, Agnes settled herself on the window seat, pulling her knees up under her chin and tucking her gown round her feet for modesty and protection against draughts. Placing her parted lips close to the pane, she breathed onto the glass with a heavy sigh, then traced patterns in the damp patch with her forefinger.

'Why are you taking William away, Nancy?' Agnes peered sorrowfully through the glass. 'I don't want him to go.'

Nancy informed Agnes a little more sharply than she intended, that William's move to Bolton was a matter for rejoicing not lament, and went on to describe in glowing terms the garret room she had arranged for his lodgings. She was securing the trunk with a stout lock when Alice appeared in the doorway carrying two feather bolsters to be added to the contents.

When all was ready the procession sallied forth in the direction of the Commercial. Nancy set a leisurely pace so that folk could admire her stylish gown of green and gold, with the overskirt trimmed in fur strips to match the flounces on the sleeves. Isabella, who liked her gowns to be pretty, but not so pretty as to attract comment or cause her to be the centre of attention, wore her favourite blue print sack-back and a bonnet with matching ribband.

Meg cared not what she wore, even if it was another's castings, so long as it did not chafe or cut into her flesh; Sarah looked delightful, as ever, in a gown she designed and stitched herself. Agnes had yet to develop her own taste in clothing.

Mrs Dawson leaned from her spinning gallery to wish the travellers a safe and speedy journey. A few steps further, old Mrs Mackereth disengaged herself from the babies she was minding and came to the window to bestow her blessings and enquire after Margaret's health. The Crackel sisters on their way to market, paused to admire Nancy's gown and wonder aloud whether it was advisable to reveal quite so much ankle. Elizabeth Moser, only days away from another lying-in, begged them to wait a moment while she fetched her set of keys, her crimson shawl and her two daughters.

They walked past a number of taverns, of which Kirkby Kendal contained an abundance, all of them overflowing with patrons it being the Cattle Fair. Isabella sought in vain to restrain her eyes from peering through the windows of these establishments.

'You shouldn't stare,' her mother told her repeatedly when she was a child. 'It's an intrusion on the privacy of others as well as being most unladylike.'

'But how else can I learn how other people live?' Isabella protested.

'Why do you need to know?' said Margaret. 'Live your own life well and leave others to live theirs.'

But Isabella simply could not resist peering into any hidden place she came across. She once peeked behind a half open door and saw a peasant cutting a dog into joints to add to the stew pot; another time she saw a woman down on her knees counting little piles of gold guineas, with such avarice the saliva dribbled from her lips.

The coaching hall was crowded and noisy. Tired mercers and manufacturers, who made the journey regularly, discussed the state of trade; inexperienced travellers, dressed in their Sunday finery, attempted to keep an eye on their boxes while attending to friends and family come to bid them farewell; would-be travellers who arrived to find tickets sold out complained loudly to their fellow passengers. The general commotion and air of anticipation left Isabella wishing she were setting out on a journey herself.

'I can see your father over there with George,' said Margaret. 'But where is William? If he doesn't come at once he'll miss the coach.'

Isabella stood on tiptoe, being short of stature, and searched amongst the throng of faces. George, pushing his way through the crowd towards them, thought how attractive Isabella was when animated and how well the blue gown suited her complexion.

'Look there he is!' Isabella waved until she caught William's eye.

When William joined the party, Andrew did his best to engage him in conversation. Rocking back and forth on his heels, he enquired how William planned to go about establishing himself in Bolton.

'I have no clear plan, sir.'

'Then tell me what you intend to do first.' Andrew put the question another way. 'What will you do tomorrow, for instance?'

'I'm as yet undecided,' William replied. His attention was given to removing the shreds of beef hash lodged between his molars, with a sliver of wood.

When the coach arrived, Nancy settled into one of the inside seats and immediately introduced herself to her fellow passengers. William bent to receive his sisters' kisses, submitted to his mother's embrace and listened expressionless as Elizabeth Moser wished him a prosperous future.

When they were done, he pulled himself up to a seat on top of the vehicle, where he would brave the elements for the sake of five shillings saved. Andrew took out a bulging purse, reached up and pressed it into William's palm.

'Thank you, sir, b-b-b-but I don't need that.' William waved the purse away.

'Couldn't you accept it to humour me?' Andrew let the purse fall into William's lap.

The coachman downed his measure of brandy and mounted his box; the horses took the strain, the wheels slowly began to turn and gain purchase on the uneven cobbles and everyone stood clear as the carriage moved off.

The depleted party began its homeward journey. When they reached the Woolpack, George invited Isabella to go with him into the garth to view the theatre recently opened there. Isabella accepted gladly; she was in the mood for new things, having just seen William depart to start a new life. The theatre was indeed impressive with its luxurious silk-lined boxes and pit filled with seats where once folk must stand.

'No doubt William will visit such as this in Bolton,' Isabella said.

'They have a theatre on every street in London,' George boasted. 'At least that's what my cousin says and he's lived twelve months in the city.' For some time he had wished to raise an important matter with Isabella and was therefore pleased to have secured an audience out of earshot of her family.

'You used to make us anxious.' Isabella smiled at the memory. 'You told us your father planned to send you there. Do you recall it? No one will send you now.'

'Does that please you?' George stamped on a piece of discarded pottery, reducing it to shards. 'Would you be sorry if I went away?'

Isabella was disquieted by the intensity of his tone. 'You know very well I would be sorry, you and Isaac are my best friends.'

'Why mention Isaac?' George's face contracted.

'Surely I stand first in your affections?'

'I have no first and last,' she insisted. 'The three of us are friends.'

George stepped suddenly into the mouth of a ginnel, pulling Isabella with him into the shadows. Then, laying hold of her hands, he enclosed them firmly in his.

'You are far more than a friend to me, Bella. I admire your composure and your wit and the sweetness of your face.' George watched for signs she reciprocated his feelings. 'I've thought about it carefully. We played together as children and understand each other perfectly. You take an interest in your father's business and in every way will make me an ideal wife.'

Isabella was dismayed; George was a dear friend but he did not stir in her the feelings a woman should have for her lover, and being a close friend should he not know this without the need for Isabella to tell him so? It struck her that she was equally guilty in that she failed to notice the alteration in his feelings towards her. And what were those feelings? Surely George could not feel for her the same passion Prince Tancredi felt for the pagan damsel.

Normally Isabella would have spoken to George openly but her mother had taught her that proposals of matrimony were to be handled with particular sensitivity to avoid injuring a man's pride. So Isabella simply reminded George his apprenticeship had four years to run, and that even then it would be a long while before he could afford to furnish a home and provide for a family.

'But we can have an understanding.' George tightened his hold and pressed Isabella against the wall so that the stones cut into her shoulders. 'You can give me your word that you'll marry me one day, once I have sufficient means.'

'I can't give you my word. Who can tell what we may be minded to do when we're older? All I can say is that, at present, I've no thoughts of marriage, to you or to anyone else.'

Isabella tried to withdraw her hands but, to her frustration, George held them firm while he continued to plead his case. She waited for as long as she considered reasonable before interrupting.

'I've listened long enough,' she said. 'And my answer hasn't altered. You must accept it, Georgie, and not make so much fuss. Now, let go my hands!'

George's jaws tightened, his lips compressed to a fine slit, his nostrils flared white-edged and, before he knew it, his hands were round Isabella's throat.

Isabella remained remarkably clear-headed. How slender and fragile is the neck, she thought, and how unprotected. How broad and strong his hands, how easy for them to snap the bones in two and twist off the head like a chicken. She looked boldly into his eyes and saw deep within him a weakness previously hidden, and loved him more dearly for it but respected him a little less.

Within a few seconds George released his grip. He examined his hands as if they belonged to another; how could he have allowed his feelings to overpower him in this way? The truth was, it never occurred to him that Isabella might fail to see the aptness of what he proposed. George was certain Andrew would give their union his blessing, as would George's own father.

Isabella arranged her fichu to conceal the redness of her neck and quickly stepped back onto the street.

'What passes for foolery between two young boys,' she said, 'can't be condoned in a grown man, and certainly not when he behaves thus with a woman.'

Isabella had seen women black-eyed and broken-boned as a result of their husband's violent chastisement, and was sickened by the sight, but she had not experienced such behaviour within her own home. Her father had not once raised his hand to wife or child; he used his voice, not force, to express displeasure and effect discipline.

George's assault did not cause Isabella to fear him, nor was she angry; her principal sentiments were pity and regret, pity that he could not control his anger, and regret that she must in future distance herself from him lest he mistake continued intimacy for a change of heart.

George apologised for his actions, which he acknowledged were indefensible, but offered no apology for his words, indeed he recommended them for her serious consideration. She had no call to be alarmed, he said; after all, she had often enough seen this anger take hold without warning, she knew it was short-lived and that his intentions were not malevolent.

Thinking to appease Isabella, George walked in front, warning her of the ubiquitous pools of cattle dung, and chasing off the scavenging dogs and swine in her path, and entertaining her by imitating a monkey with a long tail one moment and an elephant with a long trunk the next. But Isabella did not laugh and when George presented her with gingerbread, piping hot and sticky from a road side stall, she said she had no appetite.

When they reached the Paitson residence, Isabella did not enter immediately, but stood a while in contemplation.

'Let there be no more talk of marriage, Georgie,' she begged, 'else I'll cut you off altogether.'

'I promise, on my honour,' George said. 'I'll talk only of ferrit and silk and you can tell me how you teach your dull-witted pupils to do their sums.'

Entering the front room with the intention of informing her mother of her safe return, Isabella found Meg and Sarah in a state of agitation. They related how, when they were halfway home, Elizabeth Moser's pains commenced and Margaret was obliged to knock on the nearest door and ask the householder for help. Observing Elizabeth's distress, the kind gentleman led her into his foyer where she was delivered of a daughter before anyone had the wits to summon the midwife!

'And does Roger Moser give thanks his wife and infant are unharmed?' said Meg indignantly. 'No! He complains loudly that he set his heart on a son and is sorely disappointed. Can you credit it?'

'Hearing his complaint,' Sarah added, 'Mrs Moser is wailing and cursing by turns. Mamma has gone to console her because she herself has five daughters and proud of it.'

'Roger Moser should be ashamed,' said Agnes. 'Daughters care more for their parents than sons do. Look at William! He has gone away though Papa did not wish him to go.'

Isabella put her finger to her lips and shook her head. Margaret disapproved of her children speaking ill of one another.

Isabella went through to the back room where her father was dozing in his chair, his expression meek and helpless; in repose, her mother's face was quite the opposite. It acquired an air of stern authority. Isabella wondered how she herself looked when sleeping.

She trimmed the lamp and placed it on her father's writing bureau which, as usual, was strewn with scribbled notes and invoices. Selecting a quill she sharpened the point with a penknife and set to work. Initiated into the mysteries of double entry accounting by Miss Selby herself, Isabella was responsible for condensing the household accompts into neat columns of figures, recording the cost and date of purchase of every item and subtracting the sum from the allotted budget.

The process demanded her undivided attention and after the turmoil of the day afforded her relief. Andrew was wakened later by the sound of the drawer closing as, her work complete, Isabella tidied the papers away.

'Papa, how did you know whom to marry?' She came and sat at her father's feet. 'Tell me what made you choose Mamma.'

'It was her voice,' Andrew replied without hesitation. 'I was at my aunt's house, and heard your mother's voice, melodious as the ousel's song. Someone with such a voice, I reasoned, surely has a temperament to match and will make a good wife and mother to my children.'

He told the story of their courtship and subsequent marriage, a story Isabella knew by heart but which gave Papa such pleasure to relate she could not bear to cut him off. Margaret came into the room, having just returned from comforting Elizabeth Moser, and augmented Andrew's account with memories of her own, which did not always conform to his.

Isabella left them to their recollecting and slipped through the kitchen and out into the garden, where she sat quietly in the moonlight absorbing the night sounds. Ten years ago the proximity of so many neighbours was suffocating, now she enjoyed witnessing the joys and sorrows of those around her. Once Isabella saw a letter travel from Martha's bedroom, window by window along the street to her beloved's home, and his reply passed back from hand to hand in the same manner.

Having decided she could never marry George, Isabella considered what qualities her ideal husband should possess and arrived at the following list:

i   An even temperament but not too sombre.
ii   A kindly nature like Papa's and never resort to violence.
iii   Good looks though not so handsome as to attract admirers.
iv   Chivalry and passion equal to the knights in Torquato Tasso's poem.
v   The ability to incite in her a corresponding passion.

Until she met such a man, Isabella would not marry.

George was too restless to go straight home, instead he set off back towards Market Place where he hoped to find some diversion. The night was cold and the sky clear; the moon waxed full and bathed the facades lining the street in cold light. Householders on all sides barred and bolted and triple locked their doors and windows, lit their lamps and candles and stoked their fires to stave off the chill. Men congregated in taverns, some made jovial by drink while others grew morose, and a few sat alone and sought to dull their sufferings in the oblivion induced by black drops.

Women gathered round the doorway of the Pump Inn, exchanging profanities and laughing raucously. Noticing George was without a companion, one of them invited him to accompany her into a nearby garth where she would open her legs for him if he was willing to open his purse.

Sick to the stomach, George cursed her for a wanton baggage. The spectacle of these women with their garish painted mouths, and the stench of drink and rotting teeth on their breath, made him all the more determined not to give Isabella up.

CHAPTER 8

2007

The others were buzzing when they arrived and couldn't wait to tell the class what they'd found out since the previous week. Tibby sat through convoluted accounts of how they traced Aunty Ivy's mother and Grandpa Bob's long-lost brother. She didn't mind except it made her feel her progress was not worth mentioning in comparison. When it came to her turn to report she just said, 'Pass'.

Jez talked about the 1837 Registration Act and gave tips on how to order copies of certificates without getting ripped off. As before, the second half of the session was given over to practical work, this time to searching the online Census. Which wasn't a lot of use to Tibby as Isabella most likely died before 1841. She did find a couple of Peter Mosers but they were both born after 1827.

She must have looked miserable because Jez came over to commiserate.

'You're quite ambitious starting off with the eighteenth century,' he said. 'But don't give up. If you stick at it, you'll find Isabella eventually.'

'I'm not going to give up, I'm just not having much luck!' Tibby smiled and picked up this week's handout.

When she arrived home there was a message waiting on her answer machine. 'I'm just phoning to see how you got on this evening. Whether you've made any progress.' Tibby wasn't sure if Lottie meant progress on the Isabella front, or the meeting-people-and-making-friends front.

She returned the call. 'It was okay but a lot of what we do isn't really relevant to me. It's more for the nineteenth and twentieth centuries.' Tibby tried not to sound as if she was complaining.

'What did the tutor say?'

'He told me to keep trying. You can pay a professional ancestor-finder to do it for you but I'd rather do it myself if

I can.' Tibby pulled balls of fluff from her washed up her sweater. She really should go clothes shopping.

'I'd love to see it. Isabella's bible I mean.' Lottie left a hopeful pause.

'Then why not come and stay?' Tibby checked the calendar hanging above the phone. 'What are you doing at half term? Are you on childminding duty?'

'Both families are going away for the week so I should be free. By the way, the little one is doing really well. I think he looks just like his father, same nose and lips, but not everyone sees it.' Lottie continued talking about her grandchildren for the best part of an hour.

Tibby woke to a freezing bedroom. She touched the radiators. Stone cold. She went into the bathroom. No hot water. Why did central heating systems always break down at the weekend? She told herself it wasn't really a disaster. She grew up with only coal fires for heating. On winter mornings she used to scrape the ice off the inside of her bedroom window.

And what about Isabella? She didn't have a hot water tap and her house must have been freezing cold. Draughts gnawing at your ankles and ice on the bowl of water you washed your face in.

Tibby had a flannel wash at the kitchen sink with hot water from the kettle and spent a miserable couple of days with her hands stuffed into woollen gloves and nursing a hot water bottle. She caught sight of herself in the mirror, hunched up from trying to preserve her body heat, and was shocked by how old she looked.

Never mind what she grew up with, she'd got used to being warm and couldn't function properly at this temperature. Even her brain was frozen into inactivity. She couldn't concentrate long enough to read the paper or settle down to watch television. She was too cold to make the effort to go to the class. The search for Isabella's family was temporarily suspended.

The plumber announced she needed a new boiler and promised to fit one within forty-eight hours. When he didn't appear at the agreed time, Tibby phoned and was told he'd been involved in an accident.

'He's going to be in plaster for six weeks,' the woman on the other end said. 'And it might be even longer before he's well enough to come back to work.'

'Can't someone else fit the boiler for me?' Tibby tried not to sound unsympathetic.

'There is no one else. I've cancelled the order. You'd be best finding a new plumber,' she said. Then added hopefully, 'Unless you're prepared to wait?' Tibby wasn't prepared to wait. She reached for the Yellow Pages.

Altogether it was a week before the house was warm again. When they'd finished installing the new boiler she had the hottest and longest bath ever and soaked the pile of dirty plates and mugs and cutlery and promised never to take hot water for granted again.

Tibby turned once more to her genealogical research. She decided to leave Isabella for the time being and concentrate on Peter.

There were hundreds of George Mosers and Roger Mosers but hardly any Peter Mosers which narrowed it down nicely. Even better, a number of them lived in Kendal. She punched in the time frame and came up with a shortlist of two Kendal-based Peter Mosers who were old enough in 1827 to have written in Isabella's bible.

Their professions were given as cabinet maker and solicitor respectively. Solicitor! Like on the wrapping paper. It was too good to be true. What's more, this Peter Moser was born in 1800 which fitted the idea of the bible being passed from generation to generation. Tibby checked a couple of times to make sure she hadn't got it wrong then pulled the little book from its leather pouch and rested her fingertips lightly on the second inscription. She'd found the man who wrote this!

By the time Tibby rejoined the class most of the others had completed their charts and overflowed onto the continuation sheets. They'd discovered relatives they didn't know existed (the man with the tattoos was the distant cousin of the lady with the new-potato face) and the twenty year old traced her great-aunt back to the family who owned the large country house with acres of land and a deer park, a few miles outside town.

They unearthed a few scandals between them too, a number of illegitimate children and one case that looked suspiciously like incest. When it was Tibby's turn to report she told them she'd found Peter Moser and for a while she was the centre of attention as they all clapped. Good thing she went to the hairdresser that morning.

Tibby spent the rest of the week working out Peter's family tree and getting a sense of the Mosers' background. They were originally yeoman on farms around a village outside Kendal called Grayrigg (wasn't a train derailed there recently?), farms with lovely names like Craketrees, Lambert Ash, Dobbs Hole and Symgill.

Then one branch moved into Kendal, or Kirkby Kendal is it was called then, while another lot went down to London. A surprising number of Mosers were twins, unless the dates of birth were scribal errors. By the time she'd finished, the chart was looking quite healthy.

At half term Lottie came to stay. Tibby was happy enough living alone, she'd been doing it for over forty years, but she did love having someone to make a fuss of. Lottie who loved nothing more than to be cherished and coddled and generally indulged, was the perfect recipient for Tibby's fussing.

As she went round cleaning and dusting and putting things in their proper place Tibby realised how Isabella-oriented she'd become. Books on Georgian England piled up beside the sofa; *Tom Jones*, *The Vicar of Wakefield* and *Mansfield Park* on her bedside cabinet; the ancestral charts spread out on the dining table; Jez's handouts stacked on the kitchen worktop.

Lottie was delayed by heavy motorway traffic and arrived ravenous. Thankfully the dinner Tibby took such trouble over, baked tilapia with garlic butter and dill, wasn't spoiled. For dessert she served a childhood treat, grilled bananas smothered in whipped cream with a sprinkling of grated chocolate for contrasting colour and flavour, and toasted almonds flakes for crunch.

Afterwards Lottie curled up on the sofa under a duvet because in her opinion Tibby's central heating system was inadequate. As usual, Tibby fetched the album of photos taken when they were growing up. Lottie shuffled along to make space for her and they indulged in some serious reminiscing.

'I used to feel guilty,' Lottie said. 'You know, because I had a father and you didn't.'

'There was nothing for you to feel guilty about. I wasn't bothered. I was quite happy with the family I had. Dad never made me feel I didn't belong,' Tibby said.

'I know, but it's not like having a real father. Wouldn't you like to know more about yours? What he looked like. Whether he was good at writing and hopeless at sport like you.'

'And if his shoulders were double jointed?' Tibby did her party trick. 'I'd rather just leave things as they are.' The thought of those emotional first meetings with long-lost relatives they showed in documentaries, horrified her.

It was not until Lottie was sitting in the conservatory the next morning, wrapped in Tibby's cosy winter dressing gown and eating her second maple syrup pancake, that she asked to see Isabella's bible. Tibby fetched it from her study. Lottie went into the kitchen and washed her hands before touching it. She held it to her nose and inhaled its antiquity. She examined it from all sides, ran her fingers down the ridged spine and traced the gold tendrils decorating the cover.

'I see what you mean. It's beautiful! And nice to hold, solid and heavy and so small.' She opened the front page and studied both inscriptions. 'Just imagine, Isabella's hands touched this page.'

'See here, near the end where the pages don't lie straight?' Tibby took the book from Lottie. 'I think Isabella read this bit more than the rest. There's an appendix. The Psalms in rhyming verse. We had to learn psalm twenty-three by heart when I was at school. The headmistress picked on someone she didn't like and made them recite it in Assembly. I like this version better.' Tibby read aloud,

The Lord is onely my support, and he that doth me feed:
How can I then lack anything of which I stand in need?
He doth me fold in coats most safe, the tender grass fast by:
And after drives me to the streams which run most pleasantly.

Lottie asked if she could see the Moser family tree. They went into the study and Lottie listened patiently while Tibby talked her through the generational chart.

'I'd like to help,' Lottie said. 'We could go to Kendal and have a look around. You know, get an idea of where Peter lived. I don't mind driving.'

'I'd love that. We could go to the archives and look through the registers, see if we can find a record of Isabella's birth or marriage,' Tibby said. 'Not just yet though. I've got some more investigating to do first.'

CHAPTER 9

1782

Following George's unwelcome proposal and rough handling of her person, Isabella ceased to attend the daily conferences hosted by her father. She cited teaching responsibilities as the reason for her absence. Andrew was disappointed by Isabella's decision to withdraw and was at a loss to understand it; he wondered if it was linked to the sudden alteration in her attitude towards George, to whom she spoke but little and then without warmth.

'Has there been a disagreement?' Andrew enquired. 'Or some misunderstanding, between you and George?'

'I'm not a child any more, Papa,' Isabella said. 'And must be mindful of my reputation which will suffer if I appear too intimate with a young man who isn't my brother.'

Andrew was not satisfied with this answer; he himself was always present as chaperone so there could be no question of gossips' tongues or spoiled reputations. He put the same question to George.

'Everything follows the swing of a pendulum,' George said. 'Isabella doesn't wish to associate with me at present but she will when the time is right. All things have their season.'

And George truly believed this to be the case. The furze pig and the flittermouse slept in winter and awoke refreshed when the days grew warm, trees lost their leaves in autumn and were covered in new growth next spring. Isabella would eventually come round to seeing things his way.

Each day when the conference was over George found some excuse to prolong his stay, offering to run an errand for Margaret or contriving to fall into conversation with Sarah or Meg. His laughter drifted upstairs to Isabella who sat reading, and hearing it she longed to go down and join them. Oh, why could George not be content with friendship and give up the absurd notion of taking her for his sweetheart?

Isabella sought out Isaac. She walked to Bowling Fell, where grass lay beneath the feet and no dwellings obstructed the eye, and watched Isaac roll balls, slow and deliberate, across the green towards the jack. When he saw Isabella so dejected, Isaac's heart melted in his breast, but he deemed it wiser not to offer advice or interfere; in time she and George would arrive at an understanding and if they did not, well then, he would know what to do. For now he must be content to observe.

Isabella soon grew restless, for Isaac was no match for George when it came to conversation; his words trickled like Blind Beck in summer whereas George's had all the sparkle and speed of the River Kent fed by snows melting in the Kentmere fells.

One afternoon Margaret called Isabella in from the garden where she was sketching.

'Bella, take this food to the cottage on Fellside. You remember, the one where widow Capstick lives with her eight children. Alice tells me they haven't eaten in two days. Be sure to take Aggie with you to help carry the baskets.'

Though Isabella did not wish to abandon her sketch, which was just beginning to take on the likeness of its subject, she obediently changed her gown and waited in the hallway. When, five minutes later, Agnes still had not appeared, Isabella called out urgently.

'Aggie! Come quickly. It'll be dark if we delay any longer, and it isn't advisable to visit Fellside after dark.' There was no reply. Isabella ascended the stairs and came upon Agnes huddled on the window seat.

'What is it? Has something made you sad?' she asked.

'I'm short of breath,' Agnes wheezed. 'And my ribs

ache with coughing.'

'Then go and lie down and I'll tell Mamma.' Isabella touched the back of her hand to her sister's burning skin and went quickly to call her mother.

Agnes lay in bed many days aflame with hectic fever, only her feet were ice cold and no amount of pinching and pressing would warm them. Margaret applied a plaster of candle wax to her daughter's chest and spooned milk and quinine tea between her cracked lips. The smell of musty ale on Agnes' breath made Margaret suspicious, then when she saw phlegm the colour of tallow, bloody and tinged with green, she was certain. The apothecary uttered the dreaded word "consumption" and prescribed regular bloodletting and a change of air, which was out of the question as Agnes was too weak to travel.

Isabella sat at Agnes' bedside, stroking her hair, and half-expecting her to sit up suddenly, clap her hands with delight and invite them to congratulate her on the brilliance of her playacting. Andrew could not bear to enter the sick-chamber but regarded Agnes from the doorway; the sight of her face, so pale and helpless, drove an icicle of fear into his heart.

Nancy left her year-old son with her sister-in-law, took the stage coach north and arrived in time to see Agnes laid in her coffin wearing an expression which suggested death perplexed her as much as life had done.

It was too much for Andrew; Agnes gone, and William may as well be dead for all they heard from him. And dear Isabella refusing to associate with George and all the doom-laden talk of the recall of troops deployed in the Americas.

'What ails the master?' Alice said, showing Isabella a plate of food from which only two spoons-full were missing. 'He eats less than a sparrow.'

'And sleeps no more than two hours a night,' said Isabella. 'He doesn't leave the house and when neighbours come to enquire, he's overcome with emotion.'

'Yesterday I heard him shout.' Alice put down the plate so as to free her hands to add gestures to her narrative. 'And went in to see what riled him. He was standing at the mirror berating his own reflection.'

'The doctor calls it a collapse of the nerves.' Isabella did her utmost to sound cheerful. 'He says Papa will soon recover, and I believe him.'

'Let the learned doctor call it what he will,' said Alice, arms akimbo. 'But I say if you don't take care the master's brain will addle entirely. Young Dowson has been crazed in the head ever since his two sons died of the ague, both in the same week.'

Despite her own grief, Isabella knew she must set about appointing someone to take up the reins of her father's business until he revived. George was undoubtedly the most apt choice, for he knew Papa's affairs inside out; his apprenticeship had run its course, but he might agree to do it out of respect and loyalty to his former master. Isabella sent a message saying she wished to speak with George on an important matter and immediately regretted her choice of words, fearing they might be misconstrued.

When George arrived, Isabella, wearing black gown and bonnet, sat stiffly in her father's oak chair hoping to convey an air of formality.

'As you know Papa is unwell and must rest. Would you continue minding his business interests a few weeks longer, until he revives?'

'It grieves me to see Mr Paitson indisposed.' George was indeed grieved; however he was also grateful for the unexpected turn of events which promised the opportunity to heal the rift between Isabella and himself. 'Naturally, I'll continue for as long as my services are required. You had no need to ask, Bella.'

'Oh, Georgie, thank you.' Isabella's eyes filled with

tears in spite of herself. 'I couldn't manage on my own. I hoped you would agree for my father's sake.'

But it was for Isabella's sake, not Andrew's, that George took on the task. He consulted her more often than was strictly necessary and whenever possible engaged her in lengthy debate. While she was only too glad to have some occupation to distract her, she took pains never to allow George to come close, hoping to signify by this means that she welcomed friendship but rejected anything more intimate.

If George occupied the sofa which sat under the window, Isabella took the easy chair beside the fire, though her feet did not reach the floor and the seat was hollowed out where the stuffing was wanting. When he took the easy chair, she sat upon the sofa ready to jump up if he found some reason to come and join her there. If he bent over her shoulder while she perused a contract or signed a receipt, so that the roughness of his waistcoat scratched against her neck, Isabella complained he blocked the light and requested he stand back.

These manoeuvres proved unnecessary for George's behaviour was faultless and Isabella soon gave herself wholeheartedly to the daily consultations, defending her own judgements yet paying heed to George's. She admired George's single-minded pursuit of profit but disapproved the ruthless manner in which he dealt with her father's suppliers and agents, and she was not backward in saying so.

'Mr Malin came today,' Isabella reported one evening. 'His wife has the falling sickness but he can't afford the potions prescribed. I gave him the wherewithal to purchase the preparations on the understanding we'll deduct the sum from what's due to him for the next consignment of hose.'

'And what if Malin doesn't provide us with the next consignment in full?' There was an unfamiliar note of authority in George's voice. 'Who'll repay the money he owes? Are we to pay each time potions are prescribed to the cousins and uncles and aunts of one of our suppliers? You're too lenient, Bella.'

'And you're too harsh!' Isabella protested. 'It's his dear wife who is sick not some distant relation, and she didn't choose to be so.' Isabella searched George's face for signs of the compassion which previously formed part of his nature.

'If I'm strict, I am so from necessity not because it gives me pleasure. It's my duty to turn a profit, Bella, not to hand out charity. Should the business fail, all the men and women will lose their livelihoods.' George's demeanour was that of a seasoned merchant, mature beyond his years.

'Surely it's possible to be both strict and compassionate. It can't be right to fix your eye solely on profit and, for the sake of profit, neglect the welfare of those who work for you.' Isabella could not let the matter rest. 'Put yourself in Edward's shoes, Georgie. Imagine if your own wife suffered the same ailment and couldn't afford the recommended treatment. You'd be glad enough then of an employer who dispensed charity!'

'If I had a wife, which as yet I do not, and if she were unwell, I'd employ the very best doctors no matter what the cost.' George's voice was suddenly gentle.

When Margaret heard of their difference of opinion, she backed George's argument. Men could not afford to be tender-hearted; women might indulge in such sentiments within the home, she said, but in the marketplace one could give no quarter if one wished to survive.

'George is no longer a boy,' Margaret concluded. 'Like other merchants he's learned to harden his heart.' Hearing this, Isabella felt remorse at having judged George too harshly.

In due course Andrew was restored to health and resumed the management of his affairs; George continued a while in his position until Andrew was fully informed of the state of play. Then one afternoon Isabella returned from the Hospital, breathing rapidly and her cheeks aglow from the brisk walk, to find George waiting in the hallway. He was pensive and chewing his lower lip.

'This is my last day, Bella. It's time for me to strike out independently. Mr Paitson has no more need of my assistance.' George watched closely for a downward turn of Isabella's lips, a shadow in her eyes.

'Then I wish you good luck,' Isabella said, too relieved at her father's recovery to regret George's departure. 'I've no doubt you will meet with success.'

'Should you need my help in future, you only have to ask,' George replied.

Within a month of Andrew taking back the helm, hostilities in the Americas came to an end, as many had predicted, and the troops were recalled. The effect of the sudden fall in demand upon the hosiery trade was catastrophic and some merchants saw their businesses collapse entirely. Isabella wondered how her father would survive the turmoil but when she enquired he refused to discuss it, which was quite unlike his usual custom.

As the sum of money her mother had at her disposal for household expenses continued undiminished, Isabella could only surmise her father was able to make up the shortfall in income with profit from his diverse investments. Indeed this was the case initially. However, as the market deteriorated further, Andrew was forced to take loans to cover his commitments, which left his business in a somewhat precarious position, though he was loath to admit this even to himself and would divulge nothing to Isabella lest she become anxious.

The situation in Kirkby Kendal was indeed dire. The

wealthy, importuned by beggars at every turn, triple locked their doors and organised patrols to guard their neighbourhood as instances of break-in and theft multiplied. The poor shared what little they possessed with neighbours who had even less; many were driven to seek admission to the Workhouse and the Superintendent appealed to the public for donations. The vicar preached a sermon calling on his parishioners to have pity and open their hands liberally; the churchwarden took receipt of the contributions, and tipped a few coins into his own pocket for his trouble.

'A bundle of sackcloth was left on the Workhouse steps,' Alice reported. 'And inside a hapless infant too listless to open its eyes. No doubt its mother put black drops on its tongue to give her time to flee before its cries raised the alarm.'

'Poor mite,' said Margaret. 'Born out of wedlock, like as not. It won't survive, deprived of its mother's breast, and with none to cherish it. How could its mother abandon it?'

'An empty stomach drives folk to desperate measures,' Alice muttered.

'Mrs Mackereth's husband took the mail coach to Liverpool this morning,' Isabella reported. She knew of many working men who saw no other solution. 'How the children cried to see him go! One of them wailed so loud and clung so tight to his father, I was obliged to lift the child into my lap and comfort him while Mrs Mackereth saw her husband off. The poor mite was no heavier than a wooden doll.'

'I wouldn't allow anyone to leave if I had the power to stop them,' Sarah grumbled. She had already rejected three matrimonial proposals in the belief she could do better. 'There are few enough men of good breeding in the town, without depleting the numbers further.'

'This is no time to talk of breeding,' Margaret scolded.

Every morning, Isabella's pupils arrived in the classroom weak and unable to pay attention. She suspected empty stomachs were adversely affecting their progress; when she asked what they ate before coming to school, they averted their eyes so that she might not read in them the signs of hunger. Isabella sought out the schoolmaster.

'A breakfast of bread and buttermilk would improve their concentration, if you're able to provide it,' she said.

The schoolmaster agreed and appealed for funds with which to purchase provisions; the girls ate heartedly, and when they thought no one was looking, crammed chunks of bread into their pockets for consumption by hungry brothers and sisters at home.

Isabella discovered it was George who covered the cost of this venture, by charitable donation which he could ill afford; he survived the downturn only because he was prepared to accept the smallest of profit margins in order to retain the goodwill of his newly established network of customers and suppliers. Isabella resolved to thank George in person for his generosity. She found the two friends ensconced beside the river, holding a baited rod apiece, and waiting for the fish to bite. George stood up as Isabella approached.

'Bella! Come and sit with us. I don't have Isaac's patience and am already bored though we've sat here only one hour.'

'Do join us, Isabella,' Isaac said. 'But please, both of you, keep your voices low and refrain from too much movement. Else you'll scare the fish.' Isaac was reduced to offering his services as groom and driver to those who could afford to pay, there being no call for vehicles to transport goods to coastal ports as exports dwindled.

Once they had dispensed with Isabella's expression of gratitude for George's generosity, by mutual consent they avoided reference to the severe hardship facing the inhabitants of the town. Isabella sat on the bank between the two young men and they talked of light-hearted matters such as George's recent visit to a circus.

Jumping to his feet, George attempted to walk on his hands in imitation of the circus clown but toppled to the ground repeatedly. Isabella was soon wiping tears of laughter from her cheeks; she felt the years of strain between George and herself clear and an outpouring of goodwill take its place. Isaac's eyes disappeared into the smile which spread across his face as he watched them.

A little way off, a group of young lads chased one another over the brake, shouting and cheering and enjoying themselves with a carefreeness of spirit Isabella envied. She remembered the days when she raced in this very place alongside George and Isaac, and on occasion triumphed. She recalled the pounding of her heart, and the feel of spittle accumulating in her mouth, as she flew down the path with her feet scarcely touching the ground before she collapsed, breathless and exhilarated.

'How long is it since we ran like that?' Isabella indicated the group of lads. 'What do you say, will you two compete like you used to? I'll wait on the finishing line.'

'I'm willing,' George said. 'But not with you as judge; you must race with us, Bella. We'll give you a few lengths' start.' He offered Isabella his hand; if she takes it, he thought, if she willingly entrusts her hand to my grasp, it means I am forgiven.

'I accept your challenge!' Isabella allowed George to pull her to her feet. He turned away so she could not witness how great was his delight.

Isabella too was moved by the gesture; in her imagination the hand George extended in friendship finally expunged the offence he committed by the same hand more than five years earlier.

'Leave your rod where it is, Isaac,' Isabella commanded. 'You must run with us. You'll catch no fish today.' Though he had no wish to leave off fishing, Isaac complied with the request because it came from Isabella's lips.

The churchwarden turning the key in the heavy wooden door at that very moment, happened to look across to the far bank of the Kent. He saw a young hussy, revealing an unconscionable extent of leg, clamp her bonnet to her head with one hand and use the other to propel herself forward as she sped down the path with a couple of ne'er-do-wells in boisterous pursuit.

That night the warden subjected his sons to a lengthy homily on the moral decadence of youth, taking for his text the fifth chapter of the book of Proverbs.

1785

Kirkby Kendal was in the grip of a severe frost which had so far continued for ten days without respite. The townsfolk went about their business swathed in carpet rugs, their cheeks red raw and their hands blotched blue and mauve; the infirm and the aged stayed close to their fires and spread rugs over their knees and at night families huddled together for warmth.

George sat on the long bench set against the wall in the Paitson kitchen, watching Isabella beat eggs and cream.

'A man's body was found stiff and frozen half way up Entry Lane,' said Isabella, beating the mixture to a light froth. 'The landlord of the Woolpack reported seeing him leave the tavern late the previous night, the worse for drink.'

'Did you see how heavily the snow fell last night?' George said. 'No cart or wagon can pass along the highway, the drifts lie so deep. And no horse will step onto the streets.'

'Isaac says the horses can sense the ice, smooth as

glass, concealed beneath the snow.' Isabella scooped a little of the mixture onto a dish and passed it to George. 'Taste this and tell me if it needs further sweetening.'

'I must find some way to replenish my supplies of yarn.' George absentmindedly transferred a little of the eggs and cream onto his tongue before wiping his finger on his breeches. 'The looms of Kirkby Kendal lie idle. I've no income and the weavers can't earn wages to buy food for their families.'

'There's nothing to be done, Georgie. This cold spell can't last forever. You must simply wait for conditions to improve.' Isabella paused a moment, hand on her hip. 'Well, is it sweet enough?'

Alice was bent over the scrubboard. 'There are some as cannot afford to wait,' she mumbled, 'but must help themselves.'

'What's that you say?' George looked up sharply.

'I said there are some as refuse to sit and watch their families go hungry. The weavers of Fellside mean to fetch the yarn from Hawkshead market themselves.' Alice dried her hands on her greasy apron. 'They'll carry it back on sleds, the way farmers transport hay and peat across the fells.'

'But the sleds need horses to pull them. And the horses refuse to leave the stables.' George moved closer to Alice, eager to hear what she had to say.

'Horses? No, Master George, they'll pull the sleds themselves.'

'Alice, don't say such things,' Isabella scolded. 'You encourage him to act unwisely. The weavers' lives shouldn't be placed in jeopardy, their families depend upon them entirely.' But George was already planning the journey to Hawkshead with those amongst his weavers who were willing to accompany him.

Later that day the Paitson family gathered round the dining table. Alice brought in a beef pudding and placed it alongside the dish of potatoes. Heads were bowed, a brief grace intoned, and the meal commenced. As they ate, Isabella told them of George's intended trip, and of her concern for the safety of the weavers on the expedition with George who, in her opinion, was all too ready to take risks. Ladling gravy onto her plate, Margaret suggested to her husband that he might be the best person to dissuade George.

'Once George's mind is set on a course of action,' Andrew said, 'nothing will deflect him from it, no matter what arguments you raise.'

'If you can't stop George from undertaking such an enterprise, then find someone level-headed to go too,' Margaret said as she placed a slice of pudding onto Meg's plate. 'Someone who'll advise caution if they do encounter dangers on the way.'

'I doubt you'll find anyone equal to the task,' Andrew said.

The moment the meal was over, Isabella sent a message to Isaac, requesting he call on her at his earliest convenience, and within the hour he was on the doorstep.

'Do go with them, please,' Isabella begged. 'You know as well as I how foolhardy George can be. The weavers will be exposed to extreme temperatures hour upon hour, and they intend to pull the sleds themselves despite the weight. You're cautious by nature, Isaac. If you're with him, George is less likely to lead them into harm's way.'

'When did he ever heed my advice?' Isaac warmed his hands but not too close for fear of chilblains. 'If he won't listen to you, then I have little chance of persuading him.'

'He plans to cross Windermere by ferry, and the lake half frozen. He insists it's safe.' Isabella fingered the fringes of her shawl. 'Please say you'll go with them, Isaac. I can't rest for thinking some family might lose its breadwinner as a result of George's recklessness.'

It occurred to Isaac that Isabella was all too ready to

put him in harm's way for the sake of securing the safety of George and his weavers. Though he was somewhat disappointed, Isaac was not surprised, having always suspected Isabella cared more for George than for him.

'I'll go if you wish,' he said and was immediately rewarded by Isabella's grateful smile. 'But I can't promise he'll take any notice of what I say.'

The weavers assembled at the foot of House of Correction Hill, impatient to escape the confines of the town, like felons newly released from gaol. George assigned two men to each of the wide, flat-bottomed sleds and they set off through the vast white landscape.

At first, exhilaration blocked out the cold but their mood soon altered for the going was tough; the snow lay so deep it was impossible to be sure precisely where the road ran, nor could they tell what hazards might lurk underfoot.

George and Isaac pulled one sled between them; they dragged it up inclines and when they reached the crest, climbed in and descended at speed, though it was a puzzle how to steer the vehicles. George, tall and sturdy of build, was the stronger of the two and the more enthusiastic, sometimes forging ahead to show the way and sometimes falling back to chivvy those at the rear. Isaac, lean as ever, moved forward without deviation, expending no more energy than was necessary.

The weavers were accustomed to sitting all day at the loom; the effort of pulling the sleds soon sent their muscles into spasms and the bitter cold whipped their damaged chests into bouts of coughing. Sodden breeches clung to their limbs with an icy chill and despite two pairs of gloves apiece, their fingers were frozen numb, yet at the same time their bodies exuded sweat.

The well-prepared amongst them carried hip flasks and parcels of food tied up in strips of cloth, which they shared with those who came empty-handed. They scooped handfuls of snow into their mouths to quench their thirst and when they relieved themselves their steaming effluent burnt holes in the snow, then froze dark against the white. They kept themselves in good spirits by reciting bawdy verses and singing ballads with tuneful choruses.

'We're making good headway.' George beat his arms across his chest to restore the flow of blood. 'By my calculation, we should board the ferry in daylight.'

'And what if the lake is frozen by the time we arrive?' Isaac asked, mindful of Isabella's warning. 'And the boat can't pass through? It would be dangerous to cross on foot, the ice will not be thick enough to bear our weight along with the weight of the sleds.'

'Why so cautious? It's unlike you to foresee problems where there may be none!' George clapped an affectionate hand on his friend's shoulder. 'I hope you don't regret joining us?'

Isaac trudged on ahead to allow himself time to consider how best to reply, for he could not ignore the question. Isabella had not intended George to know of her conversation with Isaac, but nor had she specifically forbidden him from disclosing it. If George knew of the depth of Isabella's concern he might be more inclined to exercise caution; therefore by telling the truth, Isaac would fulfil his duty to both his friends.

'I'm under an obligation to accompany you,' he said when George caught up.

'Obligation?' George was puzzled. 'Isn't friendship reason enough?'

'Not in this case.' Isaac rubbed his hands together vigorously for extra warmth. 'I'm here because Isabella asked me to come. She summoned me last night and begged me travel with you to ensure you didn't place the weavers in danger.'

'The danger isn't as great as Bella fears,' George said, warmed by the thought Isabella had gone to such lengths to secure his safety. 'She'll see me return safely by sunset tomorrow.' He omitted to note Isabella's concern was as much for the wives and children of the weavers, as for him, and Isaac did not draw his attention to the oversight.

When the sled party finally drew near to the lake, they were cheered to see a frost fair in full swing, with skating, skittles, football, wrestlers wearing clogs, and hot food and drink for sale from hastily erected stalls, and all to the rousing music of a local band; one enterprising butcher roasted a pig on the ice.

The ferryman related how he had stayed awake all night and rowed across and back each hour to keep the channel from freezing, and demanded George pay extra for his trouble. Once on the other side, George's party dragged the sleds up to the road and at last arrived in Hawkshead where they purchased enough yarn to satisfy their need. While the exhausted weavers slept, George and Isaac sat over their ale.

'It's been a good day but taxing. And tomorrow we must cover the same ground. The sleds will run differently weighed down with cargo but no doubt we'll soon learn how to manage them.' George offered his snuff box to Isaac, who declined, preferring his own blend.

'What do you say, Isaac, Isabella has feelings for me which extend beyond friendship, has she not?' George stared into the flames.

'I cannot say. I'm not privy to Isabella's feelings.' Isaac did not wish to express an opinion on the matter though he had formed one. 'You must broach the subject with her yourself.' But George was in no haste; though his savings were accumulating, he was not yet in a financial position to give Isabella the kind of dwelling house he thought fitting. Now, in view of her appeal to Isaac, George had good reason to believe Isabella reciprocated his feelings and like him was willing to wait.

CHAPTER 10

1789

Andrew died peacefully at the age of sixty-seven. He was surrounded by his wife and daughters who, as he expired, joined hands and sang his favourite hymn. The doctor attributed his demise to chronic dropsy caused by weak kidneys and compounded by old age.

William could not be prevailed upon to attend the deathbed. However, when it came to disposing of Andrew's estate, William was obliged to put in an appearance as sole son of the deceased and co-executor of his will. William's years in Bolton had not passed entirely without success; styling himself cotton manufacturer, he enjoyed an income sufficient for his needs but not excessive. With his paunch and dewlaps, his buff waistcoat and breeches and dark green coat, he looked quite the part.

They gathered round a large oak table. The squirms and squiggles patterning the surface reminded Isabella of the stippling of sunlight passing through leaves. She sat beside her mother on one side while the three executors sat opposite. At the far end sat the attorney, a breakfast of cold mutton and boiled fowl comfortably lining his stomach, and beside him was his ink-stained clerk, whose hunger was not sated by the watery buttermilk and burnt crust served up by his landlady.

They were called to order and the reading of the last will and testament of Andrew Paitson, gentlemen and hosier, commenced. Isabella sat impatiently through the clauses dealing with real and personal estate, goods, chattels, mortgages, bonds and other securities until at last they reached the more intimate bequests. Papa promised to leave her his writing bureau but Isabella could not be certain he had recorded this in writing.

To my son William I give my silver tankard and my silver

pint, to my dear wife Margaret the remainder of my silver plate and all my books, to my daughter Nancy the round table from the back bedchamber, to my daughter Meg the small oak chest, to my daughter Sarah the set of mahogany drawers and my giltwood looking-glass, to my daughter Isabella my walnut writing bureau...

Isabella's shoulders dropped in relief. Why had she doubted him?

The attorney inserted his fingers beneath his moth-eaten wig and proceeded to scratch every portion of his scalp with evident relish. Everyone eased themselves into more comfortable positions and the men struck up conversations in hushed tones.

Nancy signalled to her three boys, who were lined up on a bench against the wall, telling them to climb down, an instruction with which they eagerly and noisily complied. Isabella lifted the youngest Jackson into her lap and swayed him gently from side to side as she hummed.

When he had scratched his fill, the attorney readjusted his wig and composed his features to match the gravity of his profession.

'Additional material has come into my possession,' he said. 'Material, I fear, of a kind which will not be welcome but which it is my reluctant duty to lay before you today.'

Silence descended as all heads turned towards him. The pleasure Isabella felt earlier on discovering her father had remembered his promise, was supplanted by a deep disquiet. She knew Papa concealed certain dealings from her over the past few years; had he done this because of their foolhardiness?

The youngest Jackson, sensitive to the change of mood though unable to comprehend the words themselves, let out a howl. He stumbled and fell as he hurried towards his mother and, in consequence, the volume of his howls increased. Nancy quickly ushered all three boys from the room, and one glance from Roger Moser sent Meg and Sarah hurrying after them. Isabella, however, announced neither she nor her mother intended to leave.

The executors conferred. Running his forefinger round inside his over-tight collar, Roger Moser expressed the view that further discussion of the deceased's finances was a matter for the executors alone. Isabella begged to differ; the matter affected the deceased's widow first and foremost, she argued, therefore her mother had the right to remain and the right to have her daughter remain with her. John Jackson gave his approval and William's silence was taken as indication he concurred, therefore Roger's objection was not upheld.

The question settled, the attorney drew their attention to an inventory of loans Andrew had taken out during recent years, citing the family home as surety. The clerk read out the precise figures while the scribbling executors added and subtracted them, then refusing to believe the result of their calculations, computed the numbers once more. The outcome was always the same, Margaret and her daughters were left with barely sufficient to cover the rent of the humblest of rooms and the cost of the simplest of fare.

Regarding Margaret with pity, Roger Moser expressed his disappointment at Andrew's failure to make adequate provision for his widow. Isabella was angered to hear her father's former friend condemn him in this way, and turned to William, certain he would redeem the family's good name.

'I don't wish to have Mamma live with me in Bolton,' he announced. 'In any case, it would be foolish to leave the town which has for so many years been her home. Naturally, I'll make regular c-c-c-contributions towards her upkeep.' Here he quoted a sum so small it deserved only ridicule.

'Would you be so kind as to tell me how you propose

to discharge your responsibilities in respect of your three maiden sisters?' Roger Moser enquired.

'If women wish to b-b-b-be treated as equal to men, then let them earn their keep as men do. Bella can open a school, she has more than enough brains for it. Meg can take in plain stitching and as for Sarah, she'll find a husband soon enough, so long as she is not t-t-t-t- too particular.' William inspected his palm, picking at a patch of thickened skin.

Hearing her son's words, Margaret turned as grey as the ash in the fireless grate. Isabella passed her the rosewater and requested a dish of sweetened tea to revive her. Isabella herself did not object in principle to William's proposals, she would like nothing better than to take in pupils, and Sarah could certainly win herself a husband if she applied her mind to it; no, it was not the substance of the proposals that disturbed Isabella, but the lack of human sentiment with which they were delivered.

Nancy entered the room apologetically and begged her husband to send for a carriage as the boys had not eaten for quite some time and were growing restless; they would have walked the distance, she said, but the weather was unfavourable. Everyone turned their eyes to the steady fall of rain streaking the window panes, of which they had until then been oblivious.

It had started raining in early summer that year, and continued, with only occasional periods of abatement, right up to Damson Saturday. Aware that further rainfall might have adverse consequences for their travel plans, John Jackson made his excuses, relieved to escape the gloomy and contentious atmosphere. William, who was to travel by the same coach, shook everyone by the hand and followed his brother-in-law from the room, insensible to, or unmoved by, the misery he left behind.

'I've said it before and no doubt I'll have occasion to

say it again,' Roger Moser declared to his wife and son when he returned home. 'There's a flaw in William's nature that stands in need of correction. You should have heard the scoundrel!' Roger eased his feet from shoes which chafed his heels and pinched his toes. 'To deny his mother shelter under his roof, and pledge such a piffling sum, goes against all that's natural.'

George had heard tell that William now spent his nights carousing in the molly-houses of Bolton, and could have disclosed the rumour. However, he had no wish to pursue the subject of William's behaviour, at least only in so far as he saw in it an opportunity to fulfil his intentions in regard to Isabella.

'Andrew Paitson, God rest his soul, indulged his children when he would have done better to follow my example and stick to the precepts of Holy Writ,' Roger continued, as he loosened the buttons of his waistcoat. 'Take George here, a better son no man in England could wish for. And why? Because I raised him according to the thirteenth chapter of the Book of Proverbs, chastising what I loved; in those pages we also read "a good man leaveth an inheritance to his children's children", an exhortation which, unlike my friend, I intend to fulfil.'

Roger spread his hands across his belly, closed his eyes and sank further into his armchair. Elizabeth looked up impatiently from her cross-stitch.

'Margaret will have to find rooms for herself and the girls as other widows do,' she said, 'if William isn't willing to accommodate them. Their house is spacious and should fetch a good price at auction.'

Roger opened one eye and stared at his wife. 'So you haven't heard? The house isn't theirs to sell, every wooden beam and every block of stone has been mortgaged, if not double and triple mortgaged. And the man had no savings to speak of.'

Isabella sat at her father's writing bureau, running her fingers along the edge of the writing flap, then up and down the drawers, flicking the handles to set them swinging one by one. How cruel that, so soon after inheriting the piece of furniture, she was sitting at it calculating the pitiful sum remaining after her father's debts were honoured.

The situation was indeed dire, whichever way you came at it. Most of the furniture would have to be disposed of by public auction, and they must find a polite establishment which let rooms at a rent they could afford.

'What will I look like when I'm living on nothing but hasty pudding?' Sarah wandered into the room, gazing at her reflection in the giltwood looking-glass. 'What will happen to my skin when I'm obliged to do the work of a servant?' She examined the softness of her hands. 'Is there no way we can keep Alice?'

'She must be dismissed,' Isabella said. 'We can barely afford to feed ourselves let alone keep a servant.'

Isabella had already explained this to Sarah a number of times. Though she was the youngest of the three sisters, the burden of making arrangements fell upon Isabella, Meg not having the wit nor Sarah the inclination to take on the task. Oh, it was too much for anyone to bear! George and Isaac must have heard the news, why had they not come to see her? Well, if they would not come to her then she must go to them.

Isabella put on her oldest pair of shoes; the moon hid behind clouds that night and in the darkness it was difficult to pick one's way through the filth. She pulled the hood of her mantelet forward until it completely shaded her face. Having decided Isaac would best answer her present need for solace, Isabella proceeded towards Highgate and thence into Kirkland, exchanging subdued greetings with townsfolk hastening home to the warmth and safety of their houses, or making their way into town to drink a gill of beer. As usual she could not resist the temptation to stare through the clouded windows of taverns at the merriment and joviality inside.

Isaac was fashioning a hound from a piece of apple wood when Isabella arrived, guiding the blade of his clasp knife with his thumb and forefinger as he pared and chamfered and cut into the grain. He put down his work and greeted Isabella with some awkwardness, then set two chairs in the yard.

Mrs Thompson brought a plate of clap-bread for refreshment, expressed her condolences and enquired how Isabella's mother and sisters were bearing up under the weight of their loss. Isabella replied, her mother was as well as could be expected and thanked Mrs Thompson for asking.

'Why does no one enquire how I am?' murmured Isabella when they were alone.

'They observe how composed you are, and don't think to ask.' Isaac studied her face then looked away into the shadows. 'You're not composed at all, are you Isabella?'

'I wasn't when I set out, but I am a little more so now.' She smiled and shivered at the same time.

'You're cold, let me fetch a shawl.'

'It's not the cold that makes me shiver,' Isabella said.

She had intended to speak of the financial predicament facing her family, and was therefore surprised to hear herself describe, instead, how much she missed her father, his gentleness and laughter and kindness towards others. She began to weep in earnest, her body was wracked by gasping sobs and her hands shook uncontrollably as she wiped the tears from her cheeks. Someone came into the yard to empty a pail of slops into the pig's trough and wished them a gruff good night.

'Why didn't you come to see me?' Isabella asked as soon as she could speak.

'Because I was at a loss as to what I should say.

George was equally tongue-tied. He's been here this evening and spoke of you.'

'And what did he say?'

Isaac recalled the conviction with which George outlined the scheme he had devised to ameliorate Isabella's circumstances. He considered warning her so that she could gather her thoughts in advance but decided that to do so would be a betrayal of George's confidence.

'I believe he'll soon tell you himself,' was Isaac's cautious reply.

George gave the forthcoming interview careful forethought, the prize was too great to risk losing. Having lived frugally for many years, he was now in possession of sufficient means to consider setting up a household of his own, and his choice of bride had not altered. His determination to wed Isabella arose from a genuine conviction they were well suited, coupled with a stubborn desire to redress the blow dealt to his pride by her earlier rejection of him.

He would address mother and daughters together, thereby avoiding the possibility that Isabella would refuse him hastily before she had thoroughly considered what he was offering, which she might do if he spoke to her alone. Moreover, Isabella's mother and sisters stood to benefit from his scheme, and could, therefore, he relied upon to further his cause by urging her to accept.

At present George was pondering the question of attire, whether it was better to appear in his fustian breeches, which were roughened and made comfortable by frequent use, or the beige woollen pair, with matching waistcoat, which might appear excessively formal. He decided upon the latter, then added silk stockings and a black hat, for the occasion was indeed momentous and warranted something out of the ordinary.

The clock struck the hour informing him he had time

in hand; too agitated to bend his mind to any other task, George went first to the White Lion where he engaged the landlady in conversation, and thence to the Paitson residence.

Alice directed George into the front room where Margaret and her daughters were already gathered; the sight of their black mourning gowns and reddened eyes served as a reminder of their grief, which George also felt, though at that moment grief was superseded by eager anticipation.

'I understand you wish to address us on some matter, Georgie.' Margaret smiled at him with genuine affection, wishing to put him at his ease for he appeared unusually excitable. 'I guess it to be a matter of some importance. You have our full attention.'

'Your misfortune weighs on my heart,' George began. 'Mr Paitson was always generous and kind to me, and I wish to do what I can to repay that kindness. I've drawn up a plan which will improve your position if you are willing to adopt it.'

George directed his remarks to Margaret but was keenly aware of Isabella's eyes upon him. He proceeded to outline his scheme, the mainstay of which was for Isabella to become his wife; this had been his cherished desire for many years, he told them, and he firmly believed it was Mr Paitson's wish also, indeed he had intimated as much. Once they were married, Mrs Paitson would be welcome to take refuge with them for the duration of her natural life.

'I'll stave off Mr Paitson's creditors.' Here George turned to Meg and Sarah. 'You may continue living in this house for a period of six months. That should give you ample time to make other arrangements. I need to secure the agreement of the executors, of course, but see no reason why they should object.' George felt sweat roll down his back; wool was the wrong choice for so mild a day.

Isabella felt as though she had just discovered the precious jewels in her necklace were nothing but coloured glass. She believed George had long since abandoned all thought of making her his wife, yet all the while he nurtured this desire in secret! Moreover, he took advantage of her misfortune and used a daughter's love, a sister's sense of duty, to entrap her.

Why had Isaac not warned her? Did George's friendship mean more to him than hers? The thought wounded Isabella as deeply as the revelation of George's plotting and scheming.

'How thoughtful and generous.' Margaret turned to her daughters. 'Are there any questions you wish to put to George? The matter concerns you most intimately, Isabella.'

'I have nothing to say.' Isabella kept her eyes fixed upon her lap.

Margaret turned back to George. 'You must grant us time to consider what you have said. If you call again after three days we'll let you have our answer.'

George walked home confident he had presented his case in a favourable light. No questions were put to him as there was no element of the plan to which they could object, he reasoned; Isabella had not met his eye because she was reluctant to reveal her true feelings for him in front of her family; and the request for time before committing themselves was a mere formality.

'It's for you to supply George with an answer, Bella,' Margaret said when they were alone. 'Consider carefully what answer you should give. Go into the garden and pick some leaves from the germander to aid your reflections. And don't forget, our situation is dire and calls for sacrifice and compromise.'

Isabella duly went outside to deliberate. George's behaviour deserved the severest censure but she could not afford to indulge her sense of outrage. Her circumstances were indeed very different from those which pertained when George first asked her to marry him, as Mamma indicated, and therefore should not her approach be different also? The course of action George proposed was beneficial to everyone Isabella loved, was it selfishness and sinful pride which prevented her from consenting? Countless sermons on the obligations of God-fearing women would suggest it was. However, Isabella was aware of other perspectives, being in the habit of reading Johnson's *Analytical Review*, which promoted a woman's right to dignity and independence of mind and condemned marriages of convenience; these notions also contributed to her thinking.

Then there was natural instinct which, she suspected, exercised more control over one's actions than intellect and religious codes; was it instinct which warned her not to accept? Or did she mistake emotion for instinct? Oh, it was all too confusing! If only there were some mathematical formula she could employ to help her arrive at a solution.

The indisputable fact remained, the sight of George did not arouse her to passion. Isabella knew this was not due to any abnormality on her part, because she had encountered men who, though not eligible or suitable for matrimony, did stir her desire. At the age of twenty-eight, there was time enough for her to find a man who could do this as well as earn her respect and provide companionship; and if she never found such a man, at least she would have the satisfaction of knowing her integrity was preserved intact.

'Isabella thinks only of herself,' Sarah complained to Margaret. 'What makes her hesitate? Does she care nothing for her own mother and sisters?'

'Consider what you say, my dear. Remember the words of scripture concerning the mote in your neighbour's eye. We complain of in others the very faults which most beset ourselves.'

'What can you mean, Mamma?' Sarah replied in an offended tone. 'I would know how to reply if George asked me to marry him!'

To divert her daughters while Isabella made up her mind, Margaret announced the house was to be thoroughly cleaned. Every item of furniture was to be dusted and polished, every floor covering scrubbed, curtains and hangings to be removed into the yard and beaten until they yielded the last speck of dirt.

The sisters were to carry out the task themselves as Alice, on the basis of the unimpeachable character provided by Margaret, was now in service to another household. The parting had been tearful and Alice insisted they promise to take her back if their fortunes rallied.

Isabella reached up on tiptoe to drape heavy bed curtains over the wall surrounding the garden, tugging and straightening until they were evenly spread. Margaret, watching from her bedroom window, thought the crewel work ugly; she had intended to purchase finer cloth and embroider it herself, but had of necessity given up the notion. Grasping the carpet paddle with both hands, Isabella beat out a rhythm until she was quite suffocated by the clouds of dust.

'Let me have the paddle.' Meg came into the yard bearing a pile of green moreen window curtains. 'You can take over once more when I'm tired.'

Meg began to thwack with slower but more powerful strokes than Isabella's. The two sisters worked on, laughing and teasing one another to lighten the task; observing their good humour, Sarah soon came to join them.

'You can help me carry the tapestry from the front room, Sarah.' Isabella leaned against the wall to recover her breath. 'It's heavy, and cumbersome to manage.'

'But it's full of spiders and nesting insects!' Sarah

squealed, appalled at the prospect.

'That's precisely why it must be beaten!' Isabella laughed.

After the tent-work tapestry they moved on to the samplers, stitched in childhood, and the other hangings, some embroidered with bright silks, others white on white. They assaulted the tall screens and the small floor rugs and even dragged the square of scotch carpet from the parlour out into the yard.

Their bodices grew damp with sweat, their cheeks red and foreheads shiny, dust and dirt covered them from their bonnets to the extremities of their petticoats, and the more dishevelled they became the more they laughed. Someone knocked the front door and Margaret called out instructions for them to wait while she descended to see who it was.

Isabella brushed the particles of dirt from her clothing and tidied her hair as she entered the room where George waited. He smiled at her unkempt appearance.

'Whatever have you been at? I won't allow you to perform servants' work when you are my wife,' he said.

Choosing her words carefully so as to not to insult or humiliate, yet vigilant she did not dilute the truth, Isabella told him she could not accept his proposal and urged him to give up the idea for she would never be his wife.

'Do you need further time to mourn the loss of your father?' George was bewildered, not having foreseen this rebuff. 'Take it. I've waited years, I can wait another six months.'

'It doesn't matter how long I delay, Georgie,' Isabella said. 'My answer won't change. If you wish to marry then choose someone else. There are plenty would readily accept.'

'Is the thought of marriage to me so abhorrent?' George's lips twisted as though he tasted something disagreeable.

'Not abhorrent. But I don't have for you the feelings a wife should entertain for her husband. I can treat you as my brother but not as my lover. '

'I could incite those feelings. You have a woman's body and a woman's needs.'

George took her hands and pressed them to his lips and when Isabella sought to free herself, he held her hands firm against his chest. She begged him to release her, but he tightened his grip. Remembering the feel of his hands at her throat, Isabella cried out in alarm. George let go his hold so roughly that she fell back into her chair.

'This behaviour is another reason why I will not consent! I will never agree to live with a man who uses his strength against me.' She nursed her bruised hands.

George acknowledged his fault and promised to overcome it; Isabella replied that was impossible, it was too deeply etched. If one day he found his dinner unpalatable, if their baby cried throughout the night, if suppliers proved troublesome and his temper was sorely tested, she was certain he would revert to the pattern of Roger Moser's rough discipline, as he had done only a few minutes previously.

'What right have you to pass judgement on my father?' said George, his livid face unrecognizable. A porcelain figure fell to the floor and smashed as he rose to his feet. 'Who are you to teach me how I should behave? Where did you get this superior knowledge of human nature which you hand down to me as if I were a child?'

'I didn't mean to pass judgement. Only to speak openly of my reasons for rejecting your offer. Please, Georgie, don't give way to anger; I hoped we could come too an understanding.' Isabella was determined not to succumb to fear, though her pulse beat rapidly and her hands trembled.

'An understanding?' George mocked. 'You'll understand well enough when you have to lodge in another's house and meet every expense by your own labour; when hunger gnaws at your belly and you have only threadbare clothes on your back; when you are forced to watch your own dear mother suffer hardship and humiliation. When you have understood this first hand, I guarantee you'll regret rejecting my offer!'

Seeing Isabella's face sickly pale, Margaret had no need to enquire what answer she had returned; nor did she quiz Isabella on the reason for her decision, though Margaret could not fathom it. Isabella liked George well enough, of that there was no doubt. What then drove her to reject his offer?

George continued without pause until he reached the White Lion. Taking his tankard of cider, he joined a group of patrons debating the extraordinary events taking place in Paris and proclaiming their support for the rebels' cause.

'Some London papers dismiss them for an unruly mob,' Capstick complained, his cheeks highly coloured and his forehead damp with sweat, 'and predict they'll soon be quelled.'

'I call them courageous men,' Batey said. 'They are intent on establishing justice where there was none. The King must be held to account.' He proceeded to denounce all royalists, and named the individual inhabitants of Kirkby Kendal he knew to be of that persuasion, which led in due course to mention of the late Andrew Paitson.

'I hear Mr Paitson's widow is condemned to live her remaining years in penury,' said Gandy, slurring his words somewhat. 'Though rumour has it someone intends to act as benefactor.'

He was referring to the conversation George had with the landlady on his way to the Paitson residence one week ago. When she quizzed George about his business, he had divulged where he was going and why and, confident of Isabella's acceptance, boasted of it rather too loudly.

'It's true.' George privately cursed the looseness of his tongue. 'And I intend to honour my pledge.'

'A generous act,' said Gandy, 'and one which deserves applause.'

They drummed their hands upon the table in appreciation of George's generosity and called for their tankards to be refilled and promptly emptied them with a toast to old fashioned chivalry. George made his excuses and walked home, his mood by turns furious and despondent.

The sale of the late Andrew Paitson's dwelling house and furniture was left principally in the hands of Roger Moser, owing to the distance at which the other executors dwelt. Offended at Isabella's treatment of his son, Roger demanded the deceased's family quit the premises at once, that the house might be sold and allow the speedy honouring of Andrew's debts. Isabella could scarcely believe her father's former friend had such scant regard for the distress this urgency caused the widow of the deceased.

Isaac experienced a moment of profound relief when he first heard of Isabella's decision to decline George's offer; a response which quite took him by surprise. Examining his heart more closely, he came to the unexpected conclusion he must be a little in love with Isabella himself. Isaac was alarmed by this thought, as he had no wish to set himself up as George's rival, yet nor did he ignore the truth.

When Isabella appealed to him to find them respectable lodgings at a reasonable rate, Isaac introduced her to Mrs Carr, the landlady of an establishment half way down the steep and narrow track running off Highgate known as Captain French Lane.

At first Margaret was appalled at the prospect of living as lodgers alongside common folk, moreover in such cheerless and unwholesome surroundings, and Isabella despaired of her making the adjustment. But when she saw there was no other way, Margaret rallied and applied all her considerable talents to making the best of their lot.

'The rooms are clean, but have a tendency to dampness being located below ground, which is taken account of in the rent.' Mrs Carr ushered them into a dismal, malodorous basement room. Although pleased to welcome lodgers who hailed from a more respectable layer of society, Mrs Carr could not resist gloating a little to see the Paitson women brought low.

'I think you'll find your fellow lodgers agreeable,' she continued. 'Single men all of them, but if you encounter any difficulties please take them to Mr Carr. You'll find him in the room directly beneath the garret.'

'I don't anticipate any difficulties.' Margaret smiled graciously. 'And hope we, in turn, will disturb no one. We'll use one room for our place of residence and one will be devoted to the use of my daughter's pupils. We're victims of misfortune, you understand, and do our best to adjust to the alteration in our circumstances.'

'My advice is to keep your chests and boxes double padlocked and to retain the keys about your person at all times.' Mrs Carr handed Margaret a set of door keys. 'Trust no one who steps across the threshold, not your fellow lodgers, nor the women who come to clean, nor the boys bringing food from the chop house, nor those who claim to be visitors.'

The basement rooms were cold, and mould decorated the walls. Isabella had no money for fuel to feed a fire so they wrapped themselves in blankets and rugs. Margaret developed a troublesome cough which no amount of syrup of coltsfoot would cure. Nevertheless she somehow contrived to provide meals for the four of them and within the tightest of budgets.

She visited the market at close of day and, for a

negligible sum, filled her bag with whatever food remained unsold. Having cultivated an alliance with Mrs Carr and gained permission to use her kitchen when she was not using it herself, Margaret boiled pans of potatoes and onions, flavoured, on good days, with mutton bones or a pig's head.

Isabella wasted no time in opening a Dame School; she sold her father's walnut writing bureau, though it broke her heart to do so, and with the proceeds ordered the carpenter to make benches for her pupils to sit upon and a plain table for herself.

She recruited pupils whose parents aspired to secure an education for their offspring but could afford to pay only a modest fee, and she devised a curriculum of spelling, grammar and arithmetic, alongside geography, book keeping and needle work. At the guardians' request she appointed an assistant who came twice a week to teach French and singing.

Isabella had long subscribed to the notion that knowledge was best acquired when associated with enjoyment, and as a result she was able to maintain discipline without resort to cane or strap. The profits were modest and not easily extracted, but Isabella was well rewarded by her pupils' effort and achievements.

The Paitson women entertained few visitors; friends and acquaintances were either embarrassed by the prospect of witnessing the family's misfortune at first hand, or unwilling to be associated with anyone who lived in such undesirable conditions. Alice came, when she could arrange to leave her workplace early, and insisted on washing down the basement walls and scrubbing the floor while she and Margaret mulled over former times.

'Remember when Agnes got it into her head to go to the cattle fair on Beast Bank,' Alice said, 'though her father forbade it? She took Mrs Dawson's youngest, saying they were going to Finkle Street to buy sugared fruits. And the

Dawson boy went straight to his mother the moment they returned, and told her the truth!' Alice laughed, a sound infrequently heard in the basement rooms.

'And the poor child couldn't sleep that night for the bellowing of bulls in his ears,' Margaret joined in the laughter. 'Mr Paitson threatened to punish Agnes but he never did.'

Meanwhile, Sarah and Meg took in sewing with limited success. Sarah stitched to perfection but with such tardiness that late delivery was a frequent complaint, while the reverse was true of Meg, who applied herself to stitching with more determination than refinement, and often enough her work was returned by dissatisfied patrons.

Isaac called in to see Isabella regularly and brought little parcels from his mother, containing chicken heads, pig's trotters, or a slice of tripe. At first Margaret was ashamed to accept these offerings but Isabella had no such qualms and was sincerely grateful for any additions to their diet.

Isaac admired the courage with which Isabella faced her altered circumstances but noticed, also, the toll it took upon her health. She must have good reasons for rejecting George's proposal, though he was not privy to them. Isabella was deeply appreciative of Isaac's visits, and not once did she refer to George's behaviour, not wishing to put Isaac in a position where he must choose.

CHAPTER 11

2007

Tibby was beginning to think she'd never find Isabella. Then one day, while she was searching the National Archives site, she came across a document from 1742 concerning someone called Andrew Paitson who lived in Kendal. He was standing surety before the court for Thomas Shearman's good behaviour.

This was exciting, the first evidence she'd come across of Paitsons living in Kendal. Andrew's profession was given as mercer which, according to the online dictionary, meant a dealer in textiles, principally silks and velvets, and he belonged to the generation before Isabella.

Tibby dug a bit deeper and found a marriage between Andrew Paitson and Margaret in Dent in 1749. She consulted the road atlas. Dent wasn't so very far from Kendal. Starting with Andrew and Margaret she did a search for their children. Only one result, Agnes Paitson born in 1763.

Agnes was born in Dent but Margaret and Andrew must have moved to Kendal later because Tibby found a record of their burials, all three of them, in the parish church. No mention of Isabella but they could be close relatives who might somehow lead her to Isabella's family.

When Tibby finished explaining all this to the class, Jez suggested she try different spellings.

'Different spellings? How do you mean?' Tibby was puzzled.

'Paitson's not a very common name,' Jez explained. 'If the clerk hadn't heard it before, he'd just guess the spelling. Or change it to something he'd heard lots of times. Like Pattison or Pattinson. I can guarantee you'll find Paitson spelled more than one way.'

There was a general murmur of agreement. One young woman claimed to have discovered a whole new branch of her family when she tried searching for Robeson without the 'e'.

'See how you get on with these.' Jez scribbled a list and handed it to Tibby.

She was tired when she got home and should have left it till the morning but she just couldn't resist having a quick look. The quick look lasted until after midnight.

Pattison, Pattinson, Patson, Pitson. Peatson, Paytson, Peytson, Pateson. Yes! There she was, Isabella Pateson born 1761 in Kirkby Kendal, to parents Margaret and Andrew. Tibby cheered aloud.

But as she stared at Isabella's name on the screen she began to feel strangely embarrassed. She'd dragged Isabella in undignified fashion from her eighteenth century surroundings and embedded her in twenty-first-century technology. Why did this online record of Isabella's birth seem to confirm her existence in a way the inscription she wrote herself didn't?

'I've found her!' Tibby told Lottie. 'I've found Isabella!'

'Excellent! Did she have sisters and brothers?'

'Ann, Margaret, William and Sarah.' Tibby read off the names. 'All of them older than her and born in Kendal before the family went to live in Dent where little Agnes was born.'

'Six of them. Hard work for their mother,' Lottie said with feeling. 'Two were enough for me. Do you have any idea how Peter fits into the picture? Why Isabella gave her bible to him?'

'Not yet.' Tibby wondered sometimes whether this would remain forever a mystery.

Inspired by her success with Isabella, she was determined to fill in as much as she could of the Paitson generational chart. Not so easy! She drew a blank with Andrew's parents and she couldn't find any of his brothers or sisters. She found Isabella's maternal grandparents but they were called Jackson which was even more common than Thompson and she quickly lost track.

Tibby took her coffee through to the conservatory where the hibiscus bloomed in scarlet splendour and purple flower heads protruded like artificial limbs from a spiky cactus. As the bitter liquid slipped down her throat, she flicked through the pages of Isabella's bible for the hundredth time, just in case she'd missed some clue. Like the archaeologists who failed to spot the arrow head embodied in the spine of the prehistoric hunter trapped in a glacier, even though they had examined the x-rays a hundred times.

Part way through the Song of Solomon, Tibby spotted some letters squeezed in between the columns. She put on her reading glasses. "I.P. & P.F." This was Isabella in love! So much in love that when she was supposed to be reading her bible, she couldn't resist writing her initials alongside her sweetheart's.

A happy innocent encounter? In those days Isabella wouldn't have the freedom to do much more than walk out with her young man. The romance didn't last of course because Isabella ended up marrying a Thompson. Perhaps her parents didn't consider P.F. suitable or perhaps he flirted with another girl and broke Isabella's heart.

All very different from Tibby's own experience. She was in her late twenties when she first fell in love, properly in love. It was an all-consuming passion which transformed her normal level-headed self into an unprincipled stranger. She did all the chasing, she couldn't deny that, flirting shamelessly with the new manager. She knew right from the start he was married, and he never promised to leave his wife so she couldn't accuse him of stringing her along.

It went on for three years; three years of dressing not according to her own taste but in styles he found appealing, of saying things she didn't mean just to impress him, of scheming and manoeuvring to ensure their paths crossed. Tibby never for an instant doubted he felt the same overpowering attraction she felt and that he dreamt of her every moment of each day as she dreamt of him. Then one morning she realised with the force of a tsunami what a fool she'd been.

It was winter and she was suffering from a heavy cold. Knowing he was booked up all day with meetings at head office, she came to work red-eyed and blotchy, without make up, her unwashed hair a mess. But the head office meetings were cancelled and he caught sight of her as she came downstairs. She saw how his jaw tightened in disgust at her appearance. He cared nothing whatsoever for her, she was simply the object of his lust. Tibby immediately requested a transfer and never saw him again.

She stood up slowly, feeling the stiffness in her back and knees. One of the action points on her personal retirement preparation plan was to join a yoga class but she still hadn't got round to it. She always stiffened up in the winter. She'd get plenty of exercise in the spring, seeing to the garden. She'd never bothered much with the garden while she was working but now she had no excuse.

Tibby wondered whether Isabella had a garden. She pictured the Paitson sisters sitting on their lawn holding parasols to protect their complexions. Or perhaps the family needed the land for hens and pigs and growing potatoes.

She found herself doing this all the time. Comparing her life to Isabella's. Did Isabella eat toast for breakfast, what books did she read if any, what did she use for toothpaste and what did she wear in bed? Tibby knew the answers to some of these questions through her reading, the others she made up by guesswork.

CHAPTER 12

1790

Word of George Moser's rejected proposal spread abroad; respectable wives gathered round their tea tables and drank Bohea from hand-painted porcelain and speculated on why Isabella withheld her consent; Dawson and Swainston took bets on how many weeks it would take for Isabella to come to her senses, now that she was mired in poverty and poor Widow Paitson with her.

George spoke to no one on the subject but grew increasingly ill-tempered and morose. From time to time he spied Isabella about her business and watched for signs of deterioration in health brought on by want of nourishment, the weariness of step and lethargy and other symptoms which were the usual consequence of a decline in fortunes.

Oh, Bella was stubborn! He should have known better than to imagine she would come round quickly to his way of thinking. George bore it for a duration of three months, during which he could apply his mind to neither the pursuit of profit nor pleasure.

When Mrs Carr announced a gentleman was asking for her, Isabella guessed immediately who it must be. She suspected George would not surrender his long-cherished ambition so easily, and she was therefore ready to reiterate her original response.

George stood in the hallway, passing his walking stick restlessly from one hand to the other with such a forlorn air that, in spite of everything, Isabella wished she could comfort him, which was not possible because the one thing which would make him happy she could not give. George registered the momentary softening of her gaze and took it for a sign her position was shifting.

'Can we speak, Bella?' He came forward eagerly. 'This chasm between us is unnatural and benefits neither of us.'

'There can be no harm in speaking, but not here. Let's go somewhere more congenial, somewhere in the open air.'

Isabella said this because she did not wish to conduct the interview in hearing of the other lodgers. George, however, took her willingness to be seen in public with him as confirmation of his earlier observation, namely that she was undergoing a change of heart.

They crossed the river and made their way to the common garden at Castle Mill and walked together along narrow paths between neat hedges bordering little diamond beds. Isabella increased her normal pace to match George's while he slowed his steps to suit hers. The sun appeared intermittently between long strips of cloud which streaked the sky; the climate was unusually mild so that folk were enticed out of their homes to take advantage of the warmth.

'How is your mother bearing up?' George enquired. 'She must find it hard to endure the conditions in which she now lives. And you, Bella, don't you pine for the comforts you formerly enjoyed?' How he longed to hear her admit she had been wrong.

'We encounter many difficulties but we overcome them,' she said. 'I have an aptitude for teaching and there's no shortage of pupils wishing to enrol. As for Mamma, she bears up well enough.'

George struck the hedge with his walking stick. She was going to hold out against him!

'You would have no difficulties whatsoever if you took up residence with me. Tell me the truth, don't you repent your decision even a little?'

'I'm in absolutely no doubt I was correct to reject your offer of marriage,' Isabella declared. 'To do otherwise would be to betray myself and to treat you unjustly. I'll not change my mind, Georgie. If you wish it, I'll remain your friend, but I'll never be your wife.' She stated her position with what she hoped was unequivocal clarity.

'You try my patience beyond endurance. I beg you, don't persist with this stubbornness.'

'You accuse me of stubbornness?' She turned to face him. 'My decision is carefully weighed and deliberated and bears no resemblance to stubbornness! I'm not a trader holding out until you bid a higher price or one whose business you can blockade till they agree to your terms. I've given you my answer in every form of words I can devise. I've nothing left to say.' Isabella made as if to leave but George blocked her path, his features contorted in fury.

'Then hear this! I'll marry your sister Sarah, who knows better than to refuse, and I'll have sons and daughters by her. But neither you, nor your mother, nor your other sisters will ever set foot in my house or come near our children!'

He brandished his walking stick above her head and Isabella feared for a moment that he would strike her. Other couples taking the air in the vicinity stopped to watch, some simply curious to know how the matter would unfold, others ready to intervene should it prove necessary. George bent down till his lips were close to Isabella's ear.

'You've brought this upon yourself, Bella. You've made a monster of me.' Then, bidding her farewell for the sake of the audience, he strode off towards Miller Bridge.

Isabella lowered herself onto a bench, hardly able to comprehend what was happening. How could George conceive of such a plan? Did he think to spite her by marrying Sarah? Did he intend to make her suffer, thinking herself to blame for the prohibition against Mamma seeing her own grandchildren?

Surely Sarah would not agree to marriage when she heard the conditions he imposed. But what if George enticed her with promises of an easy life and as many gowns as she could wear, might she then weaken? It was imperative Isabella reach Sarah in advance of George, so that she could divulge the truth about his violent behaviour. If Sarah was privy to this knowledge, she would never consent to be his wife.

Isabella walked rapidly, indeed her gait was close to running; each breath seared her throat and her mouth was dry. A rushing like ocean waves pounding the shore assailed her ears and she thought her skull must explode. She stumbled on the uneven surface and the heel of her shoe separated from the sole. The hand she stretched out to ease her fall, sustained cuts and grazes and blood seeped through the fabric of her torn glove. Immediately flies settled on the congealing mess, ignoring Isabella's attempts to flap them away.

She struggled to her feet then set off again, over the river and down Highgate. Her bloodied hand and obvious distress attracted curious glances. She panted heavily and pressed her good hand to the pain in her side but dare not lessen her speed, plagued as she was with visions of Sarah, lying bruised and beaten at the hand of a violent husband, though she told herself repeatedly this was nonsense.

As Isabella at last turned into the mouth of Captain French Lane, two figures descended the steps of Mrs Carr's lodging house and set off in the direction of the fells. Isabella called out Sarah's name and begged her to wait, but neither figure turned back. She was too late! George was even now persuading Sarah to marry him and Isabella was powerless to prevent it.   •

Seeing blood on Isabella's hand, Margaret fetched a jar of ointment.

'Hold still now, the cut is ragged and will take time to heal.' Margaret applied balm to the wound. 'Where have you been? Has something untoward occurred? George came here wishing to speak with Sarah. He seemed agitated and insisted she go with him. They left a few minutes since.'

'I saw them go.' Isabella winced as the balm touched raw flesh. 'What precisely did George say?'

'No more than that. He was determined to speak with Sarah alone and urgently. Tell me what it is that alarms you, Bella.'

Margaret sat down abruptly and rested her head against the back of the easy chair as though she would faint. Isabella fetched her scent bottle and held it to her mother's nose. As there was no way she could protect her mother from the unpleasant truth, she relayed the details of what had passed between her and George.

'Oh Mamma,' she groaned. 'I can't believe he's capable of such unwarranted perversity, such meanness of heart. And he blames me for driving him to it!'

'Sarah will be tempted to accept.' Margaret's voice was tremulous. 'She finds the endless stitching irksome and complains of the privations we endure. On the other hand, everyone knows George asked you first, Bella, and will regard Sarah as his second choice.'

'That's true,' said Isabella hopefully. 'It hadn't occurred to me; pride might lead Sarah to refuse.'

'But how would George receive it?' Margaret sat up in alarm. 'If Sarah were to deny him, he might vent his anger on her. Perhaps, after all, it would be wiser to accept.'

'Mamma! You can't think a woman should consent to marriage simply to avoid provoking her suitor's wrath. That would make me guilty of wrongdoing.'

'You made your choice. Others would have acted differently.' Margaret closed her eyes and fell back into her chair once more.

Sarah returned some time later. The brightness of her eyes and grand manner in which she conducted herself, bore witness to an event of some import. She solemnly removed her gloves and cloak, then went to study her face in the looking-glass before addressing them with a proud smile.

'You're looking at the future Mrs George Moser,' she announced. 'Georgie has asked me to be his wife and I've accepted!'

No one spoke.

'What, no congratulations?' Sarah looked reproachfully at her mother and Isabella. 'That is the customary way to receive news of an engagement. Or does your silence signify disapproval?'

'I would share in your happiness, Sarah,' Margaret said, 'but I understand there are conditions attached to George's offer, conditions I find troubling. If you're blessed with children, am I to be prohibited from seeing them?'

'George doesn't really wish it.' Sarah sought to dismiss the idea. 'He only says it to punish Isabella. Once we're married he'll relax his strictures.' She turned to Isabella. 'And I know what your objection is, Bella. He confessed he touched you in anger and has given his word never to repeat his mistake. I believe he is sincere.'

A cunning move, thought Isabella. By his confession George had succeeded in disarming her, removing the bullets from her pistol, so to speak. Undeterred, Isabella did her utmost to persuade Sarah to withdraw her consent, or at least ask for time to consider, but as she feared, Sarah would not take her account seriously, having heard it first from George. Sarah enquired caustically whether Isabella had nothing better to do than meddle in other people's lives.

'You've thrown away your chance, Bella,' she warned. 'Don't attempt to spoil mine!'

The hastily arranged wedding was a simple affair out of respect for the bride's father, who had lain in the ground not yet twelve months. George obtained a marriage bond and obliged Sarah by giving out the bride's age as two years less than the groom's, though in truth it was greater by that amount. The guests were few in number, there were no bridesmaids to escort the bride, and the Parish Church, though thoroughly swept and dusted, was not decked out.

Isaac arrived early, to find George already consulting with the vicar as to which passages from Scripture he should read. As there was no time to visit the tailor for a new set of clothes, George wore his best Sunday suit and shirt, but his tapered shoes with silver buckles were newly purchased.

'How do I appear to you, Isaac? Is there anything you would have me change?' George fingered the ruff at his neck then opened the buttons of his waistcoat only to fasten them again. 'She'll come, I'm sure of it. Sarah has more sense than to insult me as her sister did.' He chewed his lip and looked towards the door.

'She's agreed to the marriage, why shouldn't she come?' Isaac said, banishing any hint of disapproval from his voice. 'And as to your first question, I would change nothing in your appearance. Everything will go smoothly, George. You have no reason to think otherwise.'

Isaac took up his position by the main door and greeted the guests as they arrived then directed them to their pew, according to degree of affiliation and social standing. Once seated, men and women alike craned their necks time and again, curious as to whether the bride's mother and sisters would attend the ceremony. An air of restless anticipation prevailed; speculation was carried on in whispers.

'Margaret Paitson tore up the invitation. Can you believe it, her own daughter's wedding!'

'You're mistaken, no invitation was sent! George excised her name from the list.'

All the guests were duly seated and still there was no

bride. Isaac stepped out of the church and up onto the main street, but there was no sign of the carriage. He had prepared it personally and selected the horses, and given clear instructions to the driver, so the fault did not lie there. No, any delay was due to Sarah. Isaac checked the hour; she was not so very late, there was no cause for concern. George left his seat in the front pew and was halfway to the door when the bridal carriage drew up outside.

Sarah entered the church followed by William, who was to give her away. Her gown of silver hue, which she stitched herself and completed that very morning, fitted her to perfection and complemented the colour of her hair which was beautifully dressed. The congregation sighed at her loveliness, and were rewarded with gracious smiles as she processed down the aisle leaning on William's arm. George, turning to watch, congratulated himself on acquiring such a bride and quashed all thought of her sister.

'Did you ever see anything more lovely?' he whispered to Isaac. 'I've turned failure into triumph.'

'I wouldn't put it that way myself,' Isaac said, 'but I agree, Sarah does look charming.'

Bride and groom stood side by side before the vicar and plighted their troth. Elizabeth Moser wept into her handkerchief and her husband, thinking of the sum he was obliged to lay out for the wedding breakfast, felt like weeping too.

When the solemnisation was complete, Sarah slipped her arm through George's and the couple made their way back along the aisle towards the door, stopping at intervals to converse with guests. Both played their parts supremely well, and no one gave further thought to those who had a right to be present but were not.

Isaac shepherded the honoured guests into the carriages which stood waiting to convey them to Roger

Moser's residence, while those who were able, covered the distance on foot. Halfway to the destination they were met by an unruly rabble making its way toward them from the direction of House of Correction Hill. At the centre of the crowd was the wretched figure of a woman crouching in a cart, naked from the waist upwards and bearing a placard round her neck proclaiming her to be a thief.

'What is her crime?' one of the guests enquired.

'She carried off a whole cartload of peats which didn't belong to her,' cried a stout woman on the fringe of the crowd, 'and thought to get away with it. She's to be tied to the whipping post.'

'Perhaps she did it to fill her children's empty bellies,' suggested a kind hearted guest, 'or to provide them with clothing.'

'To keep herself in liquor, more like!' said another, less sympathetic.

Isaac feared the incident would be taken for an inauspicious omen and cast a shadow over the proceedings, but any such notion was soon dispelled by the mouth-watering smell of a wedding breakfast of toast, ham, eggs and tongue, freshly cooked. The meal was served in generous portions, finished off with a slice or two of plum cake and the whole washed down with cup after cup of steaming chocolate, a favourite indulgence of the groom's father. Everyone ate until their bellies were fit to burst, and drank until their lips and tongues were coated cocoa brown.

Someone ran their fingers over the piano keys for the company's amusement but no one danced or played Hunt the Slipper; as soon as their digestive organs allowed, the guests dispersed in accordance with the example set by the bride's brother, who returned straightway to Bolton without so much as passing the time of day with his mother.

The basement rooms seemed empty without Sarah; her incessant complaining and moaning, though tiresome, provided a distraction from the grim reality of daily life. Isabella quizzed Isaac as to Sarah's welfare, and kept an ear open for rumours, but she heard no adverse reports, and when she encountered Sarah in the street there were no signs of mistreatment. On the contrary, Sarah flourished and in due course provided George with a son.

'He's to be called Andrew, after your father,' Isaac told Isabella. 'I've never seen George so proud!'

'And will he allow Mamma to see the baby? Surely the sight of his own son will weaken his resolve?' Isabella knew how much Sarah would appreciate having her mother by her side at such a time.

'I've heard no mention of it; as you know George is stubborn and won't easily change his mind.' Isaac had attempted to broach the subject with George, but made no headway.

In truth, George considered Margaret a wise and loving woman, and in other circumstances would gladly have allowed her to mingle with his son to their mutual benefit, but each time he was minded to rescind his prohibition, the memory of the humiliation he suffered at Isabella's hand blocked his way. So Margaret had to be content with the occasional glimpse of baby Andrew from afar, which brought her scant comfort.

Meg was the next of the Paitson sisters to escape the gloom of the basement rooms; she announced one day she had been approached by Henry Pooley, hosier and gentleman, recently widowed and a dozen years her senior.

'He asked if I knew how to supervise the running of a household,' Meg reported to Isabella and Margaret. 'And when I said I did, he asked if I would like to become the second Mrs Pooley and take up residence in his dwelling house.'

'How very precipitous!' Margaret's lips formed a circle of disbelief. 'You know nothing of the man, and he knows nothing of you!'

'I do know a little about him,' Meg contradicted. 'I know he likes his meals to be substantial and served on time and that he is very particular about his linen. And I know he needs a wife to replace the one who died.'

Isabella made enquiries as to Henry's character and was told "the worst that can be said of him is that he wants parts" which Meg did not consider an obstacle to matrimony and therefore accepted his offer and was wed the following month. Meg called on her mother every day, bringing with her gifts of food to nourish her body and snippets of gossip to divert her mind.

Isabella herself was past the meridian of life, though not beyond childbearing; however, now that she had sole charge of her mother, she could only contemplate marriage if the man was prepared to offer her mother a home, which seemed unlikely. Unless her fortunes changed, Isabella would never know what it was to love and be loved as a woman.

CHAPTER 13

1799

'The navvies are in town again,' Alice announced. 'Brawling in the Cock and Dolphin throughout the night and none to quash them. The landlord did his best and they knocked out his teeth for his trouble.'

She added soda to the bucketful of water drawn from the well, and began to wash the basement walls clear of slime and sediment. Isabella moved the easy chair and chest a little away from the wall to allow just enough space for Alice's cleaning rag to reach behind.

'They must be canal cutters,' Isabella said.

She knew the work of those who cut the canals was gruelling; in frost and rain and sweltering midday sun they wielded their picks and spades in twelve-hour shifts with barely a break for refreshment. The canal sides must be cut at precisely the correct angle, the great mounds of surplus earth and stones dumped into waiting barrows to be wheeled away by labourers or dragged off by horses, and the raw surface then lined with puddling of wet clay and sealed by the trampling of many boots till it was watertight. The pay was generous and the food good, but the work was dangerous; more than once a canal cutter was buried alive when the sides of the channel they were digging collapsed.

'I heard they've halted work on the final section. They've run out of funds,' Isabella remarked.

'Then the navvies should seek other canals to work on.' Margaret joined the conversation from the bed where she was resting. 'Or go home, but not come to Kirkby Kendal to cause trouble.'

'They hope to find work on the roads,' Alice said. 'Which they've every right to do. Goodness knows the roads need mending. Now Miss Bella, if you would kindly wipe the walls dry, I'll carry the bucket upstairs and get rid of this foul water.' She wrung out her rag and handed it to Isabella.

'An ill-disciplined and uncivilised tribe, the Irish,' Margaret declared as soon as Alice was out of earshot. 'We must be extra vigilant.'

A web of waterways was spreading across the country, enabling the easier transportation of goods and in greater quantities. Isaac's father, Joseph, watched with trepidation fearing the advent of the barge would herald the demise of horse-drawn cart and wagon. The merchants and manufacturers of Kirkby Kendal, on the other hand, eagerly awaited the construction of the branch which would link their town to the network, so they might import coal which was in short supply, and export limestone which they possessed in plenty.

Isabella encountered a canal cutter for herself, the very next day. On her way home she peered inside the Dyers Arms at the exact moment a young man turned his face to the window, and looked deep into his eyes, though he could not see her as it was already dark. His hair grew low on his brow in the manner of her father's but his lips were fuller. Surrounded by jovial comraderie, the young man surrendered himself to the sweet notes of the Irish harp.

The sight arrested Isabella's progress and compelled her to linger. His expression, carefree and fond as a child, plucked Isabella from the shadows and set her down in a place filled with colour and light, a place free from responsibility and care. The contrast to Isabella's own life was stark; her days were so governed by duty and obligation, her waking hours so taken up with tending to her mother, management of the classroom, and matching income to expense, she had neither time nor energy for the pursuit of pleasure.

As the notes of the harp faded, Patrick Flanagan, for that was the name by which the man was known, joined in the general sigh of appreciation, followed immediately by calls for more tunes and orders for glasses to be refilled. The harpist picked up his instrument and, this time compelling it into service as a fiddle, struck up a lively reel. The inn was filled with the sound of drumming hands and tapping boots and of chairs scraped back to make space for dancing.

Patrick swayed to his feet with the idea of dancing a few turns, though the man elected to call the sets was too inebriated to carry out the task correctly. Patrick felt a pair of eyes on him and, glancing towards the doorway, saw a woman a good ten years his senior, watching him intently. She was not like the usual baggage who frequented taverns, this woman was neatly dressed and, judging by her demeanour, was well-educated. Intrigued, Patrick returned her gaze and when she did not avert her eyes as he anticipated, he went over and leaned against the door post.

'Do you have some business with me?' he inquired.

'I thought perhaps I'd seen you before.' Isabella's cheeks flushed but she held his gaze regardless. 'Were you once employed by my late father, Andrew Paitson, hosier and dealer in cloth?'

'I've never before set foot in Kirkby Kendal to the best of my knowledge.' There was a hint of insolence in Patrick's smile. 'And I know of no one who answers to the name Paitson. At least I didn't until I met you.'

'I was mistaken and apologise for troubling you. I must be on my way.' As Isabella turned to depart, she murmured, 'Perhaps we'll meet again?'

'Perhaps,' he said, brows raised and laughter rippling his bright eyes. 'Indeed I hope we will.'

Isabella's heart beat rapidly as she descended the basement stairs, and it was with trembling hands that she unlocked the door. She could still feel the heat of his body and smell his sweat. His hands were rough and his complexion coarsened by sun and wind, and yet his expression was alert and lively, and a natural intelligence lit his eyes. His only fault was lack of education and breeding, and for that he bore no blame.

Isabella consulted the looking-glass to find out how she appeared to him and was satisfied with what she saw; her skin was only here and there discoloured, her eyelids drooped a little but her eyes were clear and expressive, the lines around her nose and mouth were sparing and not too deep.

When that night she changed into her to nightgown, she noted how her waist thickened only a little when released from its corset, how in spite of her age her bosom was still shapely, the flesh on her hips and thighs still firm, her wrists and ankles still delicate and supple. Isabella closed her eyes and trembled as she imagined the brush of his skin, torn and callused from the chaffing of working tools, against her softness.

Although she did not possess a copy of *A Vindication of the Rights of Woman*, Isabella was familiar with the arguments contained within its covers and already did her best to adhere to the principles it espoused relating to the education of females. It was to the concept of "equal virtue" that she now turned, viz. the assertion that women should be judged by the same standard as that by which men were judged, in matters of physical desire and its fulfilment. Isabella was determined to apply this concept to her own condition and acknowledge unabashed that the encounter with the young man in the Dyers Arms had stirred cravings deep within her which could be neither ignored nor denied.

She returned to the tavern at the same hour on the following night and was sorely disappointed to find no sign of Patrick or his companions. As usual, a handful of women stood in the street on the lookout for the chance to earn a few coins. Their coarse, overpainted faces, roused Isabella to pity rather than condemnation.

'I have some business with one of the Irishmen who frequents this inn,' Isabella said. 'Can you tell me why they're not here?'

'There was a brawl last night.' One of the women came forward. 'It lasted two hours before they brought it to an end. Three noses broken and two jaws! The landlord's closed the doors to anyone of Irish birth.' The woman giggled, as though she was ₊privy to Isabella's secret, then spat onto the ground.

'Do you know where they might be now?'

'The Bird in Hand most likely,' another woman chipped in. 'The landlady turns no one away, indeed she notices nothing due to her liking for black drops. But you'd be unwise to follow them. It's not a fitting place for a woman of your kind.'

'You'll find the man you seek working by day on the Milnthorp road,' someone called out from across the road.

Patrick was in foul temper as he trudged back towards town. All day a steady drizzle had filled the air, slowly penetrating his garments and numbing his hands as he drove his spade through the clags of clay. Matters were not improved by the interference of the engineer supervising the work, an inexperienced and petulant young man.

The turnpike roads surrounding Kirkby Kendal were well used and therefore, as Alice rightly said, in need of constant repair; clay clogged the wheels of coach and cart in the aftermath of heavy rain, and frost left the road surface deeply pitted. From time to time gangs of navvies were sent to dig up the old road and re-lay the foundation stones before surfacing the whole with a layer of gravel.

Patrick was looking forward to a hot meal before the fire, followed by a bibulous evening. As he approached the mouth of a narrow lane running off the main street, he noticed the figure of a woman and thought her familiar. Isabella waited for him to draw near, giving him the chance to recognise her, then fell in at his side, matching her step to his.

'This weather is unkind to you,' she said. 'I trust you have somewhere to dry your wet clothes.'

'I've been out in worse than this,' Patrick replied. 'But you are wet yourself. You should take shelter.'

'I've some business to see to but will return home shortly. I hope you didn't come to any harm in the fight? I heard some of the patrons incurred injuries.' Isabella searched his face and hands for the scars of combat.

'I received no injuries myself but inflicted a few!' he said. 'The English soldiers have killed thousands of my compatriots, no wonder the men are easily roused. Do you take an interest in politics?'

'My late father was a royalist and a Tory. I myself am not well informed on the question of the Irish.' Isabella extended her hand. 'My name is Isabella Paitson.'

'Patrick Flanagan, your humble servant.' He gave the name unthinkingly, having cited it with such frequency he no longer thought its use a deception.

Patrick's given name was Peter but, since he became a cutter of canals more than a dozen years earlier, he favoured Patrick. There was not a drop of Irish blood flowed in his veins but he chose to toil and drink and brawl alongside the Catholics from Ulster because whatever they did was done with the whole heart, unlike the English navigators whom he found mean spirited and sullen.

Patrick could slip into the Irish way of speech when it suited, and had so often heard them talk, with homesick sighs, of County Antrim and Derry it was as if he had seen these places for himself. However, when it came to finding somewhere to lay his head, he preferred the dormitories of the English where he was more likely to obtain a good night's sleep.

'See, the skies have cleared.' Patrick came to a halt.

His gaze alighted on Kendal Fell. 'I've a mind to walk on that hillside tomorrow. Will you join me?' He made a little mock bow.

Next day being Sunday, Isabella attended church and was surprised to see the frieze of serpents and dragons no longer presented an awful aspect but instead seemed to frolic and cavort across the walls. Afterwards, instead of returning home, she continued up Captain French Lane, skirted the ends of the long plots to the back of Highgate and walked via Sepulchre Lane to Fellside.

Here the poor dwelt in crowded hovels with puddles of putrid waste matter congealing round the doors and the air thick with dust from hundreds of looms. Infants crawled unattended in the dirt, rats ran along the paths, and Isabella's ears were assailed by an onslaught of curses and crude expletives.

While she stood and waited for Patrick, a crowd gathered in the lane to stare. The moment Patrick arrived the discomfort was forgotten. Together they climbed through damp and shady snickets, and up steps slippery with moss, higher and higher till they reached Serpentine Woods. Patrick took care to match his manners to Isabella's, treating her with courtesy and gentleness. Where the path was rough Isabella scrambled up supported by Patrick's arm, and when she wished to rest he made a seat for her from his folded coat. He acted as her guide and showed her egg sacs suspended in spiders' webs, and cut owl pellets in two to reveal the indigestible contents.

'Look!' he said. 'A rabbit passed by not long since, see the tracks left by his paws. And see here! The blades of grass are flattened; this is where a fox lay in waiting.' Patrick crouched low and invited her to crouch beside him. 'And this is where the mice have made their nest.'

A little further on and they stood motionless, listening to the birds sing and he named each soloist as he named every grass and flower she pointed to, however insignificant, and tore the bark from fallen branches and named the insects hiding there. He even caught beetles as they scurried off and placed them in her palm to allow for closer inspection of shape and colour. Some of what he said was familiar to Isabella from her father's teaching, while some was at odds, but she did not contradict for fear of breaking the spell, for she was enchanted.

On his next visit, Isaac was surprised by the notable improvement in his friend's spirits, the radiance of her smile and the lightness of her step. He did not ask what had prompted this alteration in her temper, but guessed it and was glad, though his gladness was infused with regret.

Patrick and Isabella repeated their walk each Sunday; on the fourth week, when they reached the woods, Patrick sat astride a fallen tree and sang *Come With Me Over The Mountain* with such a degree of sincerity Isabella's eyes filled with tears. Placing his hands around her waist he drew her down beside him and asked her to sing for him; she protested she could not sing without an instrument to accompany her voice but he was in such earnest she launched into a Handel oratorio which he disliked, as he did the cantata which she sang next.

'Sing me a ballad or a lullaby,' Patrick demanded. 'Something with a heart that beats.'

'My father used to sing *Robin Hood and the Tanner* for us when we were children, but I'm not sure if I can recall all the verses.'

Isabella sang three stanzas, with Patrick thumping a lusty rhythm, before her memory failed, at which point he took up the tale and the two of them sang on in unison. He praised her voice, although she knew she could not hold a tune, and he praised the beauty of her face and the youthful proportions of her figure, which pleased her even though she knew it was for the most part flattery.

He asked her to run with him across the grass to see who was the fleetest and, when she complained the contest was unfair, he gave her an advantage but still won easily. After the race, they lay down amongst the wild flowers to regain their breath and he scattered flowers across her bosom and became intimate, murmuring loving words and caressing her, and as Isabella succumbed to his seductive charms, he in turn was excited by her virgin ecstasy.

Margaret noted a change in Isabella's behaviour; where she was formerly reliable and steady she was now unpredictable and strange. She took to whistling and bursting into peals of laughter with no obvious cause; she ran upstairs, then ran down again, having forgotten her purpose and destination; at mealtimes she paused, spoon suspended halfway to her mouth, and sat smiling to herself until Margaret roused her; in the classroom she stopped midsentence and gazed at some invisible scene until her pupils' giggles broke her reverie.

'What ails her?' asked Meg as took the potato pudding and pancakes from her basket and placed them on the table. 'She leaves Mamma unattended where before she was always at her side, and neglects her pupils which she was never wont to do. She eats like a bird and what's more sounds like one! What's your opinion, Isaac?'

'I suspect the change in habit relates to matters of the heart,' Isaac said. 'Although I haven't had the pleasure of being introduced to the gentleman in question.' He did not tell them of the rumours circulating regarding Isabella's unsavoury choice of companion.

'What, lovelorn at her age? How absurd!' Meg sat down abruptly and addressed herself to her cross-stitching.

'Remind me, my dear,' said Margaret. 'How old were you when Henry Pooley asked your hand in marriage?'

Meg looked offended for a moment then laughed

aloud. 'That's as maybe, but as I recall I did not arrange my hair in short curls and put on ridiculous gowns with waists cut so high they elevate the bosom!'

The fifth week, as usual, Isabella emerged from the Parish Church to the notes of the organ, a superb instrument, the volume and vigour of which rapidly expunged all recollection of the sermon.

A little way off a group of working men were trading ribaldries while throwing knuckle bones and dice. Patrick was amongst their number and Isabella was thrilled at the unexpected sight of her beloved, so virile and handsome in his rough coat and flat brimmed hat.

'I'd rather we weren't seen in each other's company,' she whispered when he approached. 'If you go on ahead, we can make our separate ways to the woods.'

'I'm not ashamed of my rough manners and lack of book learning but no doubt others may be,' Patrick retorted. The novelty of being with a woman on every count his superior was beginning to sour.

Isabella was taken aback by the coarseness of tone but, upon reflection, she had to admit there was an element of truth in his complaint. She had indeed thought to delay introducing Patrick to her mother and sisters until she had persuaded him not to laugh quite so loudly at his own jests and not to make quite so much noise when he took refreshment, and in general brought some refinement to his manners.

'Come with me to places of my choosing, places your acquaintances are unlikely to frequent,' Patrick suggested, more gently, and Isabella readily agreed.

The following week, he took her to the cockpit where crowds watched rival mains of birds fight to the death, but Isabella drew no pleasure from the spectacle, and another day they went to the fair and saw a bull tethered in a pit, first maddened by a burst of fireworks then set upon by dogs. Patrick cheered with the other spectators but Isabella closed her eyes, unable to stomach the sight. Patrick sensed her opprobrium.

'Perhaps a few measures of gin would induce you to give up your high minded notions of what's proper and polite, and discover some pleasure in life!' His eyes, which so recently made love to her, now regarded her with scorn. 'You seek to alter my behaviour but will not alter your own.'

How fond she was to think the gulf between his social standing and hers would be so easily bridged! He began to arrive late for their assignations, was ill-tempered throughout and found reason to curtail them. Isabella dreaded the prospect of returning to the dreary existence which was hers before she met Patrick.

'What is it that troubles you, dearest? If I've done anything to offend please tell me and I'll do my best to put it right.'

Isabella complied with his every request no matter how humiliating, she tempted him with the best meats and cakes and presented him with a snuff box and a little watch to hang upon a chain and sold her necklace to pay for them. She rubbed lard into her cheeks to lighten them, reddened her lips with vinegar and applied lampblack to her eyebrows hoping to enhance her appearance; at first she was pleased with the effect but when she caught sight of herself unexpectedly, she realised how ridiculous she looked and washed it all off again.

'I've something to tell you,' Patrick said, cleaning the dirt from his nails with the tip of his clasp knife. 'I've misled you into thinking I'm a free man when the truth is I have a wife and child awaiting my return.'

'I don't believe you!' For a moment Isabella was numb with shock, like a partridge, when the bullet finds its mark, hangs motionless in the air a moment before tumbling to the ground.

'Whether you believe it or no, it is true,' Patrick said.

'I'll not trouble you again.'

'Trouble? You have brought me joy not trouble.' At that moment Isabella would willingly have shared him with his wife, or any other woman, so desperate was she to retain his affection. She reached out to stroke his cheek but he stepped back abruptly so that her hand fell by her side.

'Tell me, Patrick, did you not love me at first?' Isabella pleaded.

'Love you?' he jeered. 'You showed an interest in me and I gave you what you desired. I know nothing of love.'

To some degree Isabella was prepared for this eventuality, that is she always knew she was entering unknown territory when she took up with Patrick, but the heart was a different question. Patrick wrenched Isabella's heart from her chest and tossed it carelessly aside; the wound was terrible and infected every aspect of her constitution. She was in the grip of a fever brought on by Patrick's announcement that their liaison was ended.

Isabella sent word to the guardians of her pupils, informing them the school was temporarily closed due to her indisposition. She took to her bed, at one moment curled up in despair, the next burning with anger at Patrick's treatment of her, yet berating herself for insensitivity and arrogance.

After two full days and nights Isabella emerged, her composure restored and her appearance as neat and orderly as before her affair, though her cheeks were a little hollower and her shoulders a little stooped. For a few months Patrick had been to Isabella all the hues of a chapman's pattern book, laughter, tenderness and the sweetness of passion satisfied. She had wrapped herself in the brilliant colours and regretted nothing. If some judged her behaviour absurd then so be it, that was the nature of love and she was not ashamed to have loved.

The years now stretched before Isabella as drab as undyed wool. Marriage was unlikely so long as her mother depended upon her to supply every need. In any case, no man could be expected to settle for tainted goods, no matter how tainted he was in his own person.

CHAPTER 14

2007

Tibby arrived early so she could pick Jez's brains. He stopped collating photocopied handouts when he saw her, and gave her his attention.

'I'm ninety-nine percent sure I've found Peter and Isabella but how can I actually prove they're the ones who wrote the inscriptions?' Tibby took out her notes and laid them on the table for Jez to see. 'I mean, it's only circumstantial evidence.'

'You're not going to find absolute proof. Not unless someone wrote it down.' Jez perched on the edge of the table and swung his jean-clad legs absent-mindedly. 'You'll have to make do with a high level of probability. What you really need is evidence of a connection between Isabella and Peter. Something to prove they knew each other.'

'What kind of something?' Tibby was wary. Jez had a habit of making things sound straightforward when they weren't.

'A marriage between a Paitson and a Moser would be best. But you'd probably have come across that by now if there was one. Or a document referring to Isabella's relatives as well as Peter's. Say as witnesses in a court case or as executors or beneficiaries in someone's will.'

Tibby thought that sounded a bit morbid, reading other people's wills. Jez contradicted her enthusiastically.

'They're full of fascinating details. One of my ancestors left his wife a black Galloway and a lock with two keys! And they can give you all sorts of clues. I can think of a few times when I was stuck and reading someone's will opened up a whole new line of enquiry.'

When the others arrived Jez filled in the attendance register. Five of the original twelve had dropped out and he warned them the class might not be allowed to continue after the Christmas break. Tibby experienced a moment of panic. Withdrawal symptoms? Someone asked the tutor if he'd continue privately if they paid him. The man with the tattoos threatened to lodge a complaint.

'You sent away for copies of Moser and Paitson wills?' Lottie asked. 'What use will they be?'

'Apparently they're full of fascinating detail and clues,' Tibby quoted Jez. 'I'm stuck so I've got to try everything.'

'Well, good luck. Let me know how you get on. By the way, my diary's getting full. We need to decide on a date for Kendal pretty soon.'

The first will Tibby opened was proved in 1759 and belonged to Roger Moser of Cracketrees in Whinfell in the Parish of Kirkby Kendal. She checked the chart. This was Peter's great-grandfather. The handwriting was beautiful but not easy to read, and the spelling was a challenge. Roger began by resigning his soul to God and committing his body to the grave. Odd, Tibby had never thought of wills as being religious.

Roger gave instructions about his messuage and tenaments and cattle and chattles, and stipulated payment of one peppercorn to the Lord of the Poor Fees! He bequeathed his desk, two featherbeds, his woollen and linen wearing apparel and a "joyners chisl" to his sons. His estate was valued at precisely £114.8.4½.

Tibby looked through a couple more. It seemed to be common practice for the executors to sell the deceased's property and possessions and invest the proceeds. Did that mean his wife was made homeless? The interest from the investment went to the wife "during her chaste viduity" which presumably meant so long as she didn't take up with someone else. One of them left his wife one guinea to pay for a Widow's Pole. The mind boggled! Ah, widow's *pall*, as in mourning clothes.

Tibby's own will wasn't half so interesting. Everything went to Lottie's two sons, except for a few small donations to charity. Her mother's will was pretty straightforward too, no mention of individual possessions. Tibby wondered whether her father had been, or was, wealthy. So far as she knew, he never paid a penny towards her upkeep, but she must have some right to a share of his estate. Banish the thought. It wasn't as though she was short of money.

She picked up the next will. It fitted the dates for Peter Moser, and his wife's name matched the name Tibby had recorded on the Moser chart. There was no doubt about it, this was the last will and testament of the man who once turned the pages of Isabella's bible. Tibby hesitated for a moment, conscious of a sense of privilege and a little reluctant to intrude.

Peter left his dwelling house in Kent Terrace and his principal monies, dividends, bonds and securities to his dearly beloved wife, Mary Elizabeth, along with all his household goods.

'Listen to this, Lottie. He wants his daughter's inheritance to be "for her own separate and absolute use and benefit, independent of any husband with whom she may intermarry." ' Tibby read the sentence into the receiver.

'Sounds like a good father,' Lottie said.

'She was his only heir. I guess things would have been different if he'd had a son as well.' Tibby was halfway through a book about the position of women in Georgian society.

For lunch, Tibby heated some soup then dozed intermittently during the special report on British troops in Afghanistan and came back to life for the weather forecast. It was the last class before Christmas, that evening. Jez had asked them each to do a short presentation, an overview of what they'd learnt and the methods they'd used, and she wanted to finish reading the wills before then. Tibby picked up the next envelope. Jez was right, wills were fascinating, even if they hadn't provided the breakthrough she needed.

William Paitson of Great Bolton, cotton manufacturer, proved 1799. The handwriting was plain and simple as was the language. William gave his clothes to the children of his brother-in-law which suggested he didn't have children of his own. Strange, there was no mention of any furniture. William's estate included property and land in Dent. Ah! That was interesting. Then came a list of his beneficiaries;

My sister Nancy wife of said John Jackson of Bolton,
bookkeeper,
my sister Margaret wife of Henry Pooley of Kirkland,
hosier,
my sister Sarah wife of George Moser of Kendal, linsey
manufacturer,
and my sister Isabella Paitson of Kendal, spinster.

WHAT! Did it really say what she thought it said? She read it again out loud this time, slowly with her finger following the words along the line. Yes! There it was in black and white. Exactly what she'd been waiting for. The missing link! She checked the ancestral charts. Peter's father was called George and his mother's name was Sarah. Very often the online records didn't give the bride's maiden name so Tibby had no way of knowing George's wife Sarah and Isabella's sister Sarah were the same person. Isabella was Peter's maternal aunt.

'I can't believe it!' Lottie was as excited as Tibby. 'And you nearly didn't send away for that one. You thought Bolton was too far from Kendal.' It was true. Tibby thought people wouldn't move that far from home but Jez told her not to discount anything and she had taken his advice.

'Presumably Isabella didn't have any children,' Lottie was still working out the implications. 'That's why she gave her mother's bible to her nephew. But she had other nephews and nieces. What was so special about Peter?'

Tibby could think of many explanations, some more realistic than others.

CHAPTER 15

1799

When the woman who did William's cleaning failed to raise him one morning, she reported her alarm to Mrs Hogg, the landlady, who came at once but likewise failed to elicit a response. They summoned Mr Hogg who, though loathe to abandon his dish of porridge, knew better than to disobey his wife. Under her watchful eye he knocked and rattled the door, calling on William to open up, but all to no avail.

'My dear, what is to be done?' Mr Hogg wiped his sleeve across the film of porridge on his lips and thought wistfully of the cup of tea growing cold on the kitchen table. Mrs Hogg solemnly handed him a weighty bunch of keys.

'Try these, Mr Hogg, though I suspect Mr Paitson has secured the door from inside by means of some device.'

'Is that wise, Mrs Hogg? We would be liable before the law in the event of theft or loss.'

'We're guilty of negligence if we do nothing. The man requires assistance!' Retrieving the keys from her husband, the landlady tried the lock herself. 'As I suspected he's attached drawback locks on the inside. There's only one thing to be done, Mr Hogg, and that's to break down the door.'

'Let's first assemble a body of named witnesses,' said Mr Hogg, spirits rising and porridge forgotten. 'A sheet of paper if you please, Mrs Hogg, and an implement with which to write!'

His wife disappeared and returned shortly with two men, one a scissor grinder, the other a peddler of brick dust, whom she had accosted in the street. The little gathering watched as Mr Hogg applied first his boot, then his shoulder, to the door a number of times with no effect other than a bout of coughing and a bruised shoulder-bone. The scissor grinder felt obliged to add his strength to Mr Hogg's, the peddler of brick dust likewise.

At this point Mrs Hogg raised an objection; could an individual be counted as reliable witness to an event if he himself partook of the action? The dispute was resolved in the affirmative, and the door eventually yielded, with a loud crack, to a combined onslaught from three shoulders.

'Lord have mercy!' exclaimed Mrs Hogg as they gazed on William's body slumped, cold and stiff, in an easy chair. 'See his book lies open upon his knee and his snuffbox at his feet.' She dabbed her eyes with her apron on seeing William's favourite blend spilled on the floor.

'And his tankard of ale sitting on the table, untouched,' said Mr Hogg, whose wife rarely permitted him to indulge in drink. 'And what have we here?' He went closer to investigate the little mounds of fish bones and nail-parings arranged along one edge of the table.

'Whatever next! I'll remove them to save embarrassment.' Mrs Hogg brushed the offending items into a square of paper and folded it to make a pocket. 'Now Mr Hogg, will you kindly inform the good doctor.'

William was forty-three years of age when he died, alone and friendless, in Bolton, the home town of Samuel Crompton who invented the Mule to spin finer thread and much more rapidly. William traded in fustian, muslin and dimity and many other fabrics besides, but his dreams of amassing wealth were never realised.

The rumours which cast him as frequenter of molly-houses and a man of lewd behaviour, were entirely false. William had for years earnestly desired to find a wife with whom he might raise a family. His failure to fulfil this wish was due to lack of even the most elementary skills of social intercourse; William simply did not possess the imagination required to step into another's shoes, which made him unfit for human companionship.

Mr Hogg was urgently dispatched to inform Mrs John

Jackson, William's next of kin, and Nancy in turn dispatched her eldest son by the next mail coach to convey the sad news to their relatives in Kirkby Kendal. Margaret was herself unfit for travel, but insisted Isabella attend the funeral in her stead; Meg elected to stay at home, as Mr Pooley was reluctant to be deprived of her services.

Isaac reserved Isabella a seat on the very next coach and accompanied her to the Kings Arms.

'You have looked drawn and weary lately,' he told her. 'It can do no harm to try a change of air.' He had noted a sudden and dramatic downturn in Isabella's mood accompanied by the onset of apathy and inertia, and concluded it was linked in some way to her recent romance.

'I doubt the air in Bolton differs much from the air in Kirkby Kendal,' said Isabella, smiling. 'But it will be good to hear from Nancy something of William's last days. We've seen little enough of him over the years.'

'He hasn't visited since your father's death, has he?' Isaac said.

'Nor corresponded,' Isabella sighed. 'But Nancy often took her sons to visit their uncle. I only wish I could have seen him one last time. '

The coaching hall of the Kings Arms, resplendent in red and yellow wallpaper, striped curtains and Turkey carpets, was brim full of bustling passengers. As ever it inspired in Isabella a mood of excited anticipation, in spite of the sad reason for the journey. Isaac went to enquire whether her coach was expected to depart on time, leaving Isabella to guard her luggage and look about her for familiar faces and in particular for the face sweeter to her than any other.

At the other end of the hall George Moser was engaged in conversation with two younger men; seeing Isabella unattended, he concluded the interview and forged a path towards her through the crowd.

'I believe we're fellow passengers.' George paused, anxious to know how she would respond. 'I assume you know, William included my name amongst his executors?'

'I wasn't aware of it.' Isabella's face remained expressionless.

'On this sorrowful occasion, can we put our differences aside and be civil with one another?' George spoke in earnest.

'I never wished it otherwise,' Isabella said. Then she added more warmly, 'I'll be glad of your company for the journey.'

Over the past decade no reports of violence on George's part had reached Isabella's ears; becoming a husband and father appeared to have mellowed his temperament. Moreover, Isabella judged George's earlier behaviour towards her less harshly now that she had herself experienced the effects of overwhelming passion.

Isaac reappeared with news of their imminent departure. The carriage was brought round and he assisted Isabella to her place. George claimed the seat beside her and was forced into ever closer proximity as other passengers arrived, laden with packages wrapped in straw, which they placed on their own knees and the knees of their neighbours and stuffed into every gap and crevice.

The assorted odours of ripe cheese, bruised damson, new leather, rancid fat and unwashed bodies, assailed the nose and Isabella took out her smelling bottle. A silver-haired gentleman announced he must have fresh air and proceeded to remove the board which covered the window nearest him; this action drew loud protest from a stout woman who demanded he replace said board immediately as the draught posed grave danger to her daughter's chest.

With no means of escape, and no other occupation, George and Isabella soon overcame any awkwardness and began to converse freely. George's account of his four sons was lovingly told and eagerly received. Andrew the first-born and image of his maternal grandfather after whom he was named, already reached his mother's shoulder in height, and was proficient in reading and wrote a beautiful hand. However he was plagued by an overly serious outlook and did not run about and play like other children.

Edward, the next in line, had no patience with learning his alphabet but inherited his mother's chestnut curls and emerald eyes, which he employed to charm everyone.

'Good looks can be both blessing and curse,' George said. 'The possession of them makes a body lazy and can lead to shallowness and vanity.' Isabella wondered whether he referred to his son or to his wife.

'Number three resembles no one but himself,' George continued. 'Young Roger is a sickly child, given to fevers and vomiting. He clings to his mother and is reluctant to come to my arms.'

'And what does the apothecary advise?' Isabella enquired, drawn to the child George so easily dismissed.

'The boy has been cupped and bled. And his mother brews potions but he refuses to drink.' George's face lightened as he told Isabella how his youngest son, John, loved to nestle in his lap and listen to one tale after another. He intimated another child was on the way.

Then Isabella asked for news of her sister, Sarah. George praised his wife as an excellent mother to their children and an admirable mistress of the house, expert in managing domestic staff and keeping the household running smoothly; in addition she was much in demand as hostess and guest at tea parties. Here he paused to stare out of the window.

'But as husband and wife, there's a deficiency.' He looked at Isabella, hoping for sympathy. 'There's no meeting of minds, no genuine communion. Do you remember how you and I shared our thoughts as children?'

'You and I and Isaac,' Isabella corrected him. 'Remember how we cut locks of hair as a symbol of our friendship? I preserved them between the pages of a little bible given me by my mother. I haven't opened the pages for years but I dare say the locks are there still. '

The silver-haired gentleman complained loudly that if he did not have fresh air at once he would faint from the overpowering smell; reaching out once more to remove the board from the window he appealed to the carriage at large for endorsement.

'And when my daughter is aflame with the ague,' the stout woman snapped, 'will you be there to mop her brow and comfort her?'

'Madam,' said the gentleman, 'it is the stench coming from your daughter that suffocates me!' This reply was met with a general murmur of agreement and a pressing of handkerchiefs to noses. The stout woman sprinkled oil of jasmine on the infant's offending nether garments.

The funeral took place in St Peter's, Bolton le Moor, a low building of no distinction to which galleries had lately been added, and the only mourners apart from the deceased's family were the two textile dealers whom William appointed co-executors, with George, of his will. They joined the family afterwards to partake of a light repast in a local hostelry. While they ate, Nancy recounted for Isabella everything she could recall of the circumstances of their brother's death.

'They say he died of apoplexy; had the doctor been summoned immediately, it is my belief William's life could have been saved. His figure was corpulent and he indulged his appetite for good food without restraint. He stayed most evenings in his room, without company. Had he conducted himself otherwise he would be alive today.'

'We all of us choose our own paths,' said Isabella, who had never seen the value of contemplating what might have been.

Nancy lowered her voice. 'I am delighted to see you reconciled with George. I trust he'll lift his cruel edict and let Mamma see her grandchildren?'

'He hasn't spoken of it.'

'Then you should raise the matter.' Nancy gave this advice with the authority of an older sister.

The menfolk ruminated on the brevity and vagaries of human life while consuming a dish of punch apiece. The mood was sombre because William died without issue, and at no great age, and George was more sombre than the others because renewed contact with Isabella rekindled his former warmth of feeling, made more poignant by contemplation of death. George imbibed copiously and when the time came for the travellers to repair to the coachhouse, he had to be supported from the room.

George and Isabella soon discovered that, due to a serious accident in which one animal lost its life and two others were injured, no horses were available to pull their coach until the morrow. The inconvenienced passengers issued strident demands for overnight accommodation and the beleaguered landlord insisted, with equal vigour, that every bed was already taken and the best he could offer was a cushion apiece and space to lie down on the floor.

'Leave this to me, Bella,' George said, rising unsteadily to his feet. 'I'll see to it you have somewhere comfortable to lay your head tonight.'

'The carpet will do well enough,' Isabella assured him. 'In any case I'm not ready for sleep. My mind would not settle.'

But George insisted on going in search of the landlord and was absent some considerable time during which Isabella occupied herself in reading the volume of verse by

Charlotte Smith she had discovered on the shelves of the subscription library, a collection of poems remarkably in tune with Isabella's present melancholic mood. She turned to *Huge Vapours Brood Above the Clifted Shore*, her favourite so far.

> *All is black shadow, but the lucid line*
> *Marked by the light surf on the level sand,*
> *Or where afar, the ship lights faintly shine*
> *Like wandering fairy fires, that oft on land*
> *Mislead the pilgrim; such the dubious ray*
> *That wavering reason lends,*
> *In life's long darkling way.*

Isabella savoured many other poems in the book, and was about to settle herself as comfortably as possible on the carpet for the night, when George came lurching towards her.

'Come, my dear. I've secured a place for you. It's tiny, more like a cell than a room, but will afford you some privacy.' George collected their possessions and, issuing a command to follow, made his way unsteadily back along the corridor from which he had earlier emerged.

Isabella hesitated, George in his cups was not the same man as the George who conversed with her on the outward journey. So long as they were overlooked she was not in danger but the place to which he was now taking her was private and hidden away.

George disappeared round a corner and, anxious not to lose sight of her bags, Isabella hurried to catch up. The room, when they reached it, was extremely small and totally devoid of ornament. It contained one bed and nothing else besides. George inspected the mattress and, having satisfied himself it was not infested with bugs, ushered Isabella inside.

'We'll have to make the best of it,' he said, 'and share

this bed for the night. There can be no harm in it. I'll place these bolsters between us. '

Isabella took in the portly figure, the thinning hair, the coarse complexion, and felt affection rather than alarm. In any case she was by now too weary to protest. George lay flat upon his back, arms by his sides, in the style of a monarch, and was sleeping soundly in a trice; Isabella lying beside him, drew surprising comfort from the rhythm of his snores.

The mattress was not conducive to slumber, being hollowed out in places and bulky in others. Isabella had not long fallen into a light sleep when she was wakened by the weight of George's arm flung across her upper body. Attributing no importance to the incident, she turned onto her side dislodging the offending limb, but was soon disturbed again, on this occasion there could be no doubt, with deliberate intention. Isabella sat up abruptly.

'Wake up, Georgie! You mistake me for Sarah!' she cried, thus giving him the opportunity to desist and retain his honour, but George chose not to avail himself of her generosity. Instead he incriminated himself still further by taking her hands and kissing them.

'I don't mistake you for anyone, my dearest. You have more passion in your fingers than your sister has in her entire body. Sarah is blessed with beauty but she's lukewarm when we lie together, and has been from the outset.'

'You can't expect me to make good her failing!' Isabella drew back her hands sharply. The touch of his lips on her skin was nauseating to her, as was the smell of his breath; she feared she would gag and vomit, and reveal the extent of her revulsion.

'I can't expect it, but I can ask.' George let go her hands and began to stroke her hair. 'And if you're generous and kind, Bella, you'll give me what I ask.'

Isabella shuffled hurriedly towards the edge of the

bed but George enveloped her in his arms and pressed her tight against his chest. This was unjust! He knew she could not match him for strength. If she screamed for help, the matter would become public and Sarah would hear of her husband's indiscretion, which Isabella wished to avoid. So she begged George to consider how shameful were his actions, but he heard only the urgent voice of his desire.

'Just this one time, Bella, please,' he begged. 'It can do no harm as no one will hear of it.'

He peeled back Isabella's skirt and petticoats to expose the shift she wore next to her skin then began to fumble with his own clothing. Desperate to free herself, Isabella struggled with a strength beyond that which she normally possessed, while George, weakened by the consumption of liquor, struggled to restrain her.

'God's blood!' he said breathlessly. 'Would you die a virgin, never having felt a man's yard move within you?'

'But I *have* known a man, Georgie. And what's more I carry his child as proof. I will not give birth for another five months so the baby is not yet visible from without, but I assure you I do not lie.' Isabella pressed George's hand down onto her belly, though all her instincts rebelled against the act. 'Do you feel the swelling?'

The first month her flowers failed, Isabella barely noticed, being consumed by her passion for Patrick; the second month she thought her body held back the flow of blood out of grief for his jilting of her; the third month Isabella lost her appetite and noticed an unfamiliar sensation in her breasts.

It was Widow Gelderd, a resident of Sandes Hospital and former midwife, who recognised the symptoms. She asked Isabella to lie on the bed and proceeded to probe her body and soon concluded Isabella's womb had quickened at least twelve weeks. She recommended an infusion of rue and penny royal and if that failed she offered to extract the unwelcome material with pincers. Hearing this, Isabella came close to fainting and had to remain on the bed until her head cleared. Declining the widow's kind offer, she hurried away as fast as she could.

At first George was too shocked to make any sense of Isabella's announcement; then he thought it must be a ploy to prevent him fulfilling his desire. But the expression on Isabella's face convinced him she told the truth so he removed himself to the foot of the bed, recoiling from her sinful flesh and from the bastard it enveloped. But even his condemnation of her was short lived, soon the idea took hold that Isabella had fallen prey to some villain, and was an innocent victim who merited pity not censure. Now George rose to his feet and cursed Isabella's seducer, demanding she reveal the blaggard's name.

'I was neither misused nor seduced,' Isabella asserted, 'but acted entirely of my own will. I was the one who approached him and I agreed to everything that happened.'

'That's impossible!' George raised a hand to block out what she told him. 'You only say so to defend him. But you needn't be ashamed. A vile scoundrel has taken advantage of you. Tell me who he is, Bella, and I'll see to it he wastes no time making you his lawful wife.' George leaned towards her, drunken spittle dribbling down his chin.

'He can't marry me within the law. He already has a wife and children.' Isabella failed to mention that Patrick did not inform her of this fact until he had grown tired of her, for to portray herself as victim of Patrick's deception would only serve to increase George's anger.

'May heaven's everlasting fury strike him!' George roared, 'I swear by Almighty God I will discover who he is and when I do, God help us all. I'll thrash him for what he has done to you. The rogue shall not live to do the same to another woman.' He drove his fists into the wall.

Isabella cried out she loved the father of her unborn

child and did not wish him harmed in any way.

'You *love* him? Yet you could not find it in your heart to love me, who would have married you?' Tears collected in George's red-veined eyes.

'We cannot chose whom we love,' Isabella whispered.

CHAPTER 16

1799

George woke to a throbbing pain which threatened to split his skull asunder, a bilious stomach and vague, intermittent memories which slowly presented themselves in increasing and unpalatable clarity as the morning wore on. First to take solid form was the unwelcome, but indisputable, fact that Isabella was with child; next he recalled treating her roughly in his attempt to extract the name of the infant's father.

He could not recollect precise details but observed, with foreboding and disgust, that his hands were grazed and a little swollen. Other more disturbing memories hovered like dark shadows on the periphery of his vision and, even at that distance, turned his bowels to water.

When the coach arrived George occupied one of the seats on top. There, fortified by frequent resort to his hip flask, he brooded amidst the drizzling rain which persisted throughout the morning. As the damp, grey miles passed by, so George's desire for vengeance, or the redress of wrongdoing towards a blameless woman, as he preferred to denote it, increased in strength until it became an unshakeable resolve. All that remained was for him to determine by what means to effect the redress.

Isabella, meanwhile, passed a feverish night possessed by a single thought, namely that she must warn Patrick of George's malevolent intentions and urge him to leave the area immediately. Every muscle, every nerve, in her body was trained towards this one aim and would remain so until it was accomplished.

George had robbed her of dignity and forced her to reveal what she would have kept secret. He threatened the one she loved, and reviled the unborn child who was the product of that love. She had forgiven George much, but this she could not forgive.

'Are you unwell, my dear?' The woman sitting opposite leaned forward and tapped Isabella's knee. 'Your face is deathly pale and you seem on the verge of fainting. Here, come and sit by me.' She began to rearrange her luggage so as to make space.

'The uneven motion makes my stomach churn.' Isabella placed her hand on her belly and prayed that George's roughness had caused no harm to the infant lodged there.

The other passengers began to dispute the recent practice of fitting steel springs to the underside of coaches to make the ride more comfortable, which one party favoured on the grounds they were no longer jolted and thrown about inducing fear of broken bones, while the opposition complained the up and down motion caused bouts of nausea, as evidenced by Isabella at that very moment. Isabella closed her eyes and prayed for Patrick's safety.

When they reached Kirkby Kendal, George disembarked and, without taking leave of Isabella, went straight to knock on Henry Pooley's door. Meg greeted George with surprise and pleasure, informing him her husband was from home. Her appearance was vastly improved, indeed one hardly noticed the pox scars owing to the glow of contentment which radiated from her.

'My business is with you, Meg, not with Henry.' George rubbed the crust from his bloodshot eyes. 'If you will allow me inside, I will explain.'

'You're welcome to enter our home, though I don't know how I can be of help. Do you come straight from the coach house? I heard the Manchester coach was delayed.' Meg disappeared briefly to instruct her servant regarding refreshment.

George first satisfied Meg's curiosity in regard to William's funeral then tried to establish whether she knew the identity of Isabella's seducer; it was soon evident her knowledge was even more limited than his own, and for the main part based on rumour and conjecture. Meg had reason to suspect her sister had taken a lover, though Isabella would neither deny nor confirm it, but she did not know the man's name nor had she gleaned any clue to his identity.

She seemed to be ignorant of the condition of Isabella's womb and George refrained from mentioning it. It did not occur to Meg to wonder why George took such an interest in Isabella's personal affairs or whether there could be any harm in discussing them so freely.

'And now tell me about my nephews,' said Meg, taking up a more pleasing theme. 'I will not allow you to leave before you have given me a full account of each one!'

George went next to the Thompson's house where, finding Isaac abroad, he passed the time in meaningless exchanges with Joseph who had been robbed of his reason by the shock of his beloved wife's death. If left unguarded, Joseph would roam the streets in search of his mother, thinking himself to be a child of seven years not an old man of seventy, and had more than once been relieved of his purse by some unscrupulous fellow.

On his return, Isaac ordered Martha, who now saw to household matters, to bring a plate of cold mutton and dish of gooseberry wine. George, who ate sparingly but drank more than his fair share, came straight to the point and asked whether Isaac knew that Isabella had come under the influence of a most unsuitable fellow.

'I noticed a change in her mood,' Isaac said. 'And suspected she had an admirer. As she did not confide in me I did not think it my business to ask. Isabella is as free to choose her companions as you or I and does not require guidance.'

'That was always your failing, Isaac. You would rather let things be than intervene. Well, you would have done well to intervene on this occasion. Bella's judgement was clouded and the villain got the better of her and now she carries a bastard in her womb, and the father a married man! She told me so herself.' George smote the table with his palm, causing Joseph to jump a clear six inches out of his chair. 'Now do you understand what spurs me on?'

'I'm grieved to hear of it. I had no inkling.' Isaac was deeply troubled by the unexpected revelation. 'But I cannot conceive of Isabella doing anything against her will. She knows her own mind and does what is right according to her own heart, no matter what others think of her.'

'Then you believe her capable of knowingly taking up with a man who already has a wife?' George spoke with rising anger. 'And allowing him to be intimate? Impossible! She yielded under duress.' He spat through the open window. 'I'm determined to find the scoundrel and punish him as he deserves. You can go with me if you like, Isaac, otherwise I'll go alone.'

It occurred to Isaac it was not so much a desire for justice which drove George, but the knowledge that another had been where he could not go. Perceiving George was in no condition to discuss the matter calmly, Isaac agreed to meet him first thing the following day and help track down the father of Isabella's unborn child. He hoped that come the morning, George's head would have cleared so that he might be reasoned with and dissuaded.

Martha came into the room bringing fresh lamps, their wicks trimmed and their glass chimneys cleaned of soot; Isaac asked if she had heard rumours concerning Miss Paitson.

'I have heard she was seen walking on Gooseholme with a young man half her age,' Martha said, proud to be able to supply the information. 'An Irishman, by all accounts.'

'Idolatrous papists! Let me at them!' Joseph shouted and, rising to his feet, began to throw punches in the air.

Then dropping to a conspiratorial whisper, he said, 'That was mere subterfuge. Bring them to me, the poor persecuted wretches, they will find asylum in my house.'

'There are no Irishmen here presently, sir.' Martha guided Joseph back to his chair. 'But if I see one I will direct him to you.'

'You must be mistaken,' said George with a frown. 'There have been no Irish gentlemen visit these parts so long as I can remember.'

'Gentlemen? Who speaks of gentlemen?' Martha played the trump card with relish. 'The man seen arm in arm with Miss Paitson was nothing but a common navvy!'

George's zeal for vengeance was equalled by Isabella's determination to forestall him. Alighting from the coach, she returned briefly to Captain French Lane to satisfy herself her mother wanted for nothing. She washed her face and hands and tidied her hair and in general restored to her appearance a semblance of composure, then, under the pretext of being charged with the delivery of an important communication, Isabella extracted from Mrs Carr a list of establishments which did not turn away the Irish, as many were wont to do.

Isabella arrived at the first address and proceeded up the path, stepping over the wall-eyed cat which lay in a patch of sun licking a suppurating sore. Two children were ensconced in the doorway, the girl rested her head in her brother's lap while he trawled through her tangled locks searching for lice. He caught them as they scurried across her scalp and held up each one for his sister's approval before squashing it between two stones; the eggs adhering to her hair he picked off and crushed between his thumbnails.

Isabella requested the children to call whoever was in charge. They ignored her request but, by good fortune, the landlady of the establishment noticed Isabella and came to speak with her.

'Patrick Flanagan? No one by that name resides here at present, though the name is common enough. Two men answering to it lodged here six months ago, the occasion of much confusion!' The landlady looked at Isabella with curiosity. 'And might I be so bold as to ask your business with Mr Flanagan?'

Isabella said she was not at liberty to disclose her business, but thanked the woman for her help and made her way back past the children who had swapped positions; the girl now plucked lice from her brother's head and tossed them to the cat.

The landlord of the next lodging house informed her a man by the name of Patrick Flanagan occupied a room in the garret; Isabella was overjoyed and followed the landlord eagerly up the stairs, wondering how she might convince Patrick his life was indeed in danger. They waited while the occupant turned keys in a number of locks and the door eventually opened to reveal a man with a red beard and but a single tooth in his lower jaw; he regarded Isabella with great surprise while she regarded him in confusion. The landlord mistook their mutual regarding for the self-consciousness of lovers, and quickly retreated, leaving Isabella to apologise and make her exit alone.

Had Isabella but known it, the adjourning establishment, which accepted only men of English stock, bore the name of Peter Mason on its list of current lodgers which was the name bestowed on the man she knew as Patrick as an infant, with the sign of the cross.

Even as they spoke Peter Mason, alias Patrick Flanagan, was in the yard washing off the day's dust and mud before sitting down to devour the beef pie he had purchased on his way home. Had Peter not taken a liking to the Irish and changed his name, Isabella would have found him and warned him in time to make good his escape, and all that happened subsequently might have been avoided.

As it was, Isabella continued to pass from lodging house to lodging house, repeating the same question and receiving the same denials and expressions of sympathy. She was not disheartened; if Patrick was yet in the town she would find him, and if he had already moved away, well then he was not in any danger. Having drawn a blank at every lodging house on Mrs Carr's list, Isabella set off home to rest briefly and take refreshment, before venturing forth once more to search this time amongst the inns and taverns.

In the event, Mrs Carr met Isabella at the door with the news that Mrs Paitson had fallen following a sudden turn. No harm was done beyond bruising to the leg, but Isabella was obliged to spend the evening at home rubbing a balm of rosemary oil and nettles on the swollen limb and in general providing comfort. Had she been free to trawl the hostelries, she would have found Patrick, or Peter, in the Dyers Arms, conversing with one of the maids who had taken his fancy.

But as it was, she could only hope George would return to Sarah tonight, and not pursue Patrick until the following day, by which time she would have sought Patrick amongst the teams of navvies repairing the roads and warned him of George's intent.

George made slow progress along Highgate, turning Martha's outrageous assertions over in his mind. The rascal was half Isabella's age, which if taken literally would mean the man had not yet attained his twentieth year. Impossible! More likely he was thirty at the very least, but had the semblance of youth, being strong and of a lively disposition. Martha described him as a navvy, indicating he was a man of the inferior kind; nevertheless the fellow must also display a certain refinement, a degree of polish, else Isabella would not be drawn to him. A native of Ireland, Martha had said, a conjecture based upon his mode of speaking, which probably meant no more than that the fellow did not speak in the local accent.

George peered into the face of every labourer he passed in the street, tortured by the thought that these thin, cracked lips or those ones, full and pendulous, had kissed Isabella's lips, and these bright, mischievous eyes, or those dark and lugubrious, had gazed with counterfeit love into hers.

He listened intently to the cadence of their speech and soon came across two fellows conversing in an accent which he recognised as Irish, and fell in behind the pair, and followed them to the Bird in Hand where he occupied the table adjacent to theirs, facing away from the light to avoid recognition.

At first the men were wary of George's questions, but the more liquor they swallowed the less guarded they became. When George pressed them, they admitted they had heard rumours of an English woman's ardent pursuit of one of their number, a man answering to the name of Patrick.

George swore that whoever spread the rumour was mistaken; Patrick was the one in pursuit and the English woman his victim. He refilled their dishes and they told him they had a notion where Patrick could be found.

'This is yours to pocket if you convey a message to him.' George drew two half guineas from his purse and laid them on the table.

'What's the message, sir?' they asked, without taking their eyes off the coins.

'Tell him he will hear something to his advantage, if he goes immediately to Miller Bridge.' George's voice was low and gruff. 'A certain gentleman will wait for him there.'

CHAPTER 17

1799

Sarah touched the back of her hand to the forehead of the child curled up on her knee; as she feared, the fever burned more fiercely. She debated whether it was better to summon Dr Askew at once or wait until her husband returned. George had little patience with young Roger's weak constitution, and might object to incurring further expense.

It was damp and overcast, the children had been confined to the house all day and Sarah devoted herself to entertaining them so they would not become fractious before George returned. He frequently indulged his children, laughing and playing with them in the way her father had done, but at other times George used his own father as a pattern and applied discipline with a strictness Sarah considered too harsh, including application of a schoolmaster's birch.

Thankfully, George had never once raised his hand in anger to Sarah herself, contrary to Bella's predictions. If some act or word of Sarah's enraged him, he would march from her presence and not appear again until his wrath had cooled.

Andrew, the eldest boy, came into the room followed by Edward and John, hand in hand. All three looked at their mother defiantly.

'Why is Papa so late?' Andrew asked. 'Liza says it's time to put us to bed but we won't sleep until we know what Papa has bought us from Bolton.'

Sarah glanced at the clock standing in the corner of the room; afternoon had already passed into evening and still no sign of George. She was expecting him to return the previous night until news of the coach's delay reached her from the Kings Arms.

Sarah hoped the sadness of the occasion and the

length of time George and Isabella were spending in each other's company would result in a reconciliation. Then perhaps George would give permission for Mamma to meet her grandsons; she laid her hand on her belly, a granddaughter also, if her instincts were correct.

Sarah would not raise her daughter as she herself had been raised. Her parents taught her she was beautiful so she played the part, first as coquette and later as elegant wife; Isabella on the other hand, according to their father, possessed a fine brain, so he gave her to supervise the household accompts, and she went on to be schoolmistress and spinster.

For many years Sarah felt she was the more fortunate, but as her own children grew, she found herself unable to satisfy their curiosity and wished she had better knowledge of the wider world. Her conversations with George were limited to household affairs, and he never sought her advice regarding business or debated with her the merits and defects of Vicar Robinson's sermons.

Recently, Sarah overheard Mrs Roxbury express the opinion that women who filled their heads with trifling matters of beauty and fashion, as found in the pages of *The Lady's Magazine*, were ill equipped to nurture their children's minds or earn their husband's respect as equals. Not that Sarah approved all Mrs Roxbury's opinions, some she found repugnant, for example, the notion a woman might determine the productivity of her own womb; the church held the view, based on Holy Writ, that every child was a gift from above and to gainsay this was most surely blasphemy.

'Papa sits me on his knee and tells a story.' John, the youngest, began to sob. 'I won't go to bed without my story.'

Sarah lifted Roger from her lap, though who was in a high fever and clung to her and whimpered pitifully; she passed him to Liza with instructions to sponge his brow and wrap him well.

'And when he is in bed, send for Dr Askew,' Sarah instructed. Then she took a book from the shelf and beckoned to her remaining sons. 'Let's sit on the couch. I will read you The Tragical History of the Children in the Wood.'

Looking across from where he was standing on Miller Bridge, George could just make out the neat pattern of Castle Mills gardens opposite, the low land of Little Aynam downstream, and upstream the ghostly shape of tenters frames haunting Gooseholme island. Two men wished him a curt good night as they crossed the bridge on their way home. George opened his hip flask, though his head was already befuzzled.

He was assailed by a plethora of odours; smoke from household grates and kitchen ranges and tallow candles, the stench of earth closets, kitchen middens, piles of rotting horse dung and the nauseating smell of the tanpits. It had not rained for two weeks, and the water was thick with noxious waste from the upstream mills.

This area of town was congested; the long, narrow burgage plots originally intended for the growing of food and housing of domestic animals, were now built over with warehouses, household dwellings, butteries, stables and workshops, all pressed together as tightly as warp and weft.

The yelp and snarl of dogs fighting over scraps, the grunt of swine in their sties and lowing of cattle in shippons, the muffled cries of children and mumbled conversations, interrupted by the all-pervasive textile workers' cough, gradually subsided with advancing night, to leave only the sound of the dark waters breaking against the piers and the quiet plash and plop of vermin moving about in the river.

George might have called Patrick out and appointed

seconds, with pistols as his weapon of choice, but the Irishman belonged to the lower sort judging by the vulgarity of his companions, aside from which, George himself was not the duelling kind.

A considerable period elapsed and he began to think his message had not been delivered or that Patrick had not taken the bait on account of cowardice; George was on the point of abandoning his vigil, when a figure emerged from the gloom, advancing with a sprightly gait and humming to himself. George, with every muscle taut and all faculties sharpened, stepped forward and demanded to know the stranger's name and business.

'I'll tell you my name if you first tell me who's asking,' Patrick replied, his head full of the carnal delights promised by the pretty barmaid waiting for him in the Dyers Arms.

'A true and trusted friend of Isabella Paitson,' was George's prompt response.

'And who might she be?' Patrick spread his hands in fake ignorance.

Enraged by the man's flippancy, George moved closer, ready to block any attempt at escape. 'An innocent woman you have taken advantage of, as you very well know!'

'And why not? Show me a man worthy of the name who would turn his nose up at a roasted goose, even a stringy one, laid out on a trencher and beckoning to him!' Patrick chuckled and stretched his arms as if to indicate Isabella lying before him.

'How dare you!' George roared. 'Have you no respect?'

Lunging forward, he dealt a blow to the jaw which caught Patrick completely by surprise, and sent him staggering backwards against the low parapet; before he could recover his balance George came at him again, this time landing a blow to his midriff which left him doubled up and breathless. In reply Patrick grabbed George's arm and wrenched it high behind his back till he grunted with the pain. George twisted free and attacked once more.

A punch from Patrick split George's upper lip and another cut him above the eye; George's fist bloodied Patrick's nose and cracked his cheekbone. Each man struggled to overpower the other; Patrick, the younger and, after so many years spent labouring, the stronger, should have enjoyed the advantage, but George was seized with devilish anger which infused him with unnatural strength.

Time and again Patrick had his opponent fast and called on him to surrender, and on each occasion George came back at him with renewed ferocity. Both men were drenched in sweat despite the cold but neither would give way.

'What would your wife say ... if she saw you so passionate ... in your defence of Isabella?' Patrick goaded his adversary, panting heavily.

The arrow struck its mark but instead of distracting George, the notion Sarah might hear of the matter spurred him on; with a growl he locked his elbow around Patrick's neck and squeezed until the navvy was begging for mercy.

'Did you show mercy when you abandoned Miss Paitson with your unborn child?' George demanded between clenched teeth.

'Child?' Patrick's surprise was genuine. 'She never told me.'

'So the fault lies with her, does it?' George drew Patrick's head back as if he would crack the bones in his neck. 'She might have told you if you were not in such a hurry to leave.'

Desperate for air, Patrick clawed at the arm constricting his windpipe then threw his weight this way and that trying to knock George off his feet. As the minutes ticked by Patrick's head seemed to detach itself from his body and float away; barely conscious, he slumped to the ground. Only then did George loosen his hold.

'You will leave this town first thing tomorrow and never show your face here again.' George's voice was thick with emotion. 'I will find out if you try to return, and next time I will not spare you. Understand?' Patrick moaned his acknowledgement.

The thud of hooves accompanied by voices warned of an approaching vehicle. George hurried down to the river and splashed the blood from his face and hands, then made his way home, leaving Patrick to come to his senses in his own time.

Isaac rose early as arranged and waited until mid-morning but George failed to put in an appearance, so he made his way to Captain French Lane to enquire whether Isabella had any news.

A group of Isabella's pupils was gathered in front of her door, debating noisily amongst themselves whether to wait longer or return home where they would be obliged to mind their younger siblings and set metal teeth in cards and undertake other chores they would rather not perform. Mrs Carr fluttered round them, wringing her hands and complaining loudly of their want of discipline and lack of consideration for others.

'Mr Thompson! I am so pleased you're here! Kindly advise me what I should do. They arrived for lessons as they do each morning, to find Miss Isabella absent and Widow Paitson refusing to provide an explanation.'

'As they're already here, then let them stay. I'll teach their lessons until Miss Isabella returns. Kindly open the door to their classroom.' Isaac had never tried his hand at teaching but was prepared to put himself out for the sake of Isabella.

Comfortably seated at the teacher's desk, he

proceeded to relate the tale of Gulliver's adventures enlisting the children to take the part of the Lilliputians, then, as Isabella still had not appeared, he embarked on Robinson Crusoe, casting himself as Man Friday.

As she descended the stairs, despondent and weary, Isabella was surprised to hear Isaac's voice coming from inside the classroom and even more surprised to discover her pupils gathered round quite transfixed by his performance. Truly, he was a man of hidden talents.

Later, when the pupils were dismissed, Isabella provided Isaac the same explanation she had given Mrs Carr earlier, an account they both knew to be less than the truth. Neither of them referred to Isabella's predicament yet the knowledge of it filled the air and stifled conversation.

'Remember, Isabella, you can always come to me if you're in need of help.' Isaac took her hand and enclosed it for a moment within his, which was something he had never done before, nor had he ever addressed her with such tenderness.

CHAPTER 18

1799

A lad on his way home from one of the tanyards noticed a substantial object fetched up on the bank at Miller Close and, being of a curious disposition, crossed over to take a closer look. The body had been in the water some time; the stomach was distended and the eye balls rotten.

Greed being more powerful than revulsion, the lad removed two silver rings from the corpse's fingers, though the skin was puckered and beginning to come loose from the bones. He did not sell the rings immediately but kept them safely hidden until the commotion abated. He would have taken the boots also but the legs and feet were so bloated from immersion, no matter how hard he tugged he could not loosen them.

When she heard they had found a body in the river, Isabella guessed immediately who it was and, dismissing her pupils early, sat alone in the classroom contemplating the news. Though she had no hope of reviving their former intimacy, Isabella took pleasure in the knowledge that somewhere Patrick woke and laboured and laughed and slept, even though she could not see him. Now, bereft of even this small measure of comfort, Isabella was overwhelmed by a fierce desire to protect and foster the tiny scrap of life lodged within her, which was all that remained of Patrick. She went directly to Meg's residence and related as much as was necessary of the events of the recent days.

'George came to the house and quizzed me about your private affairs.' Meg picked at her nails. 'I took it for idle curiosity. Now you tell me he had a hidden purpose! But why ask me? I didn't know the name of your sweetheart, nor anything about him.'

'George thought you did, and hoped you would let slip some detail which would lead him to Patrick.'

'Then he was less than honest.' Meg stood up. 'I'll come with you right away and see what he has to say for himself.'

The discovery of Patrick's body filled George with foreboding; what if someone who saw him with the two Irishmen in the Bird in Hand provided the authorities with a description? Or supposing someone observed the fight on the bridge? George was not guilty of murder, but he was guilty of something equally abhorrent. Isabella was the only one who could attest to it, though to do so she must reveal her own secret.

George was therefore unnerved when Betty announced his wife's two sisters were standing on the doorstep, demanding to speak with him. He ordered her to lead them to the parlour where he indicated they should sit on the sofa opposite the window, and endeavoured to appear offhand as he enquired their business. Isabella's dark-ringed eyes stared defiantly at him as she put her case.

'I say you tracked Patrick down and quarrelled and fought, and this encounter cost him his life. These injuries provide further evidence. How do you account for them?' She pointed to the abrasions around George's knuckles, the weeping cut above one eye and swollen lip.

'An assault by a drunken rascal who mistook me for his enemy.' George gave the answer he had prepared for the authorities. 'I have the names of two bystanders who witnessed the attack. Both are willing to give evidence under oath.' He stuck his thumbs casually in his waistband.

'And how much will you pay your witnesses to clear your name?' Isabella jeered. 'They deserve a handsome reward for misrepresenting the truth!' She could hardly believe George capable of uttering such falsehoods; it grieved her that he should sink so low, and it grieved her more that she too was forced to resort to plotting and scheming to achieve her purpose.

'You took an uncommon interest in Bella's private affairs on your return from Bolton.' Meg took up the cudgels. 'And now I know why; you planned to use what I told you, in all innocence, to seek him out and do him harm.'

'I don't deny I wished to find the man.' George's calm and reasonable manner was in sharp contrast to the impassioned words of his accusers. 'I was displeased at his treatment of Bella and wished to recommend he leave the area at once. But I had no intention of causing him bodily harm.'

'Displeased? Recommend? You were enraged and threatened dire punishment. I remember word for word the oaths you swore and the curses! How can you so flagrantly deny what you know to be true?'

Sarah heard her sisters' voices coming from the parlour, and surmising George had lifted his prohibition, hurried eagerly into the room, John perched on her hip and Roger in tow. Sensing something amiss, she came to an abrupt halt and looked from one occupant to another seeking an explanation. George made no attempt to disguise his irritation.

'Meg and Bella are here on business that doesn't concern you, Sarah,' he said. 'Now take the children and leave us to finish our discussion.'

Sarah regarded him coldly and without fear. He dismissed her as though she were a person of no consequence, the way he might dismiss a child or a servant. According to Mrs Roxbury, a husband should always address his wife in the manner he would use when addressing an equal.

'It's not for you to say what is, and what is not, my business.' Sarah set John down on the floor, and sent him off, hand in hand with his brother, to ask Liza for a

177

palmful of sugar each.

Isabella was encouraged to see her sister so emboldened; for her plan to work, she needed Sarah as her ally. George, on the other hand, was alarmed by his wife's rebellious words, which were quite out of character. However, with Isabella and Meg present, he was reluctant to upbraid her, and instead gave his attention to the fire, prodding the smouldering slabs of peat till they sprouted flames.

Sarah turned to Isabella. 'Will you tell me, as my husband will not, what matter is so pressing that you and Meg have come here without stopping to change your gowns or cover your heads?'

Isabella related the facts surrounding her accusation, as she had done to Meg a little earlier.

'Something is lacking,' Sarah said when the tale was told. 'George may have regretted, even despised, your entanglement with the Irish navvy, Bella, but that alone wouldn't drive him to violence.'

'I can tell you his motive.' Isabella leant forward eagerly. 'I entered the liaison willingly, and told George as much, but he was convinced that I was coerced. It was the desire to punish my so-called abuser which drove him to commit murder.' Isabella loosened the fastening of her gown, then eased the garment from one shoulder to reveal a line of contusions turning from purple to green. 'I received these marks at George's hand because I refused to disclose the name of my lover and father of my child!'

All eyes focused on the small, round bruises, each corresponding to one of George's fingertips. The sight appalled and disgusted George, but he continued to prosecute his own defence, now with increased vigour.

'No one will believe the allegations you level at me,' he scoffed. 'I'm known as an honest and upright gentleman, and generous in my donations to the needy.'

'And I swear you're a liar!' Isabella was herself

surprised at the assiduity with which she hounded him. 'I say you were possessed by the violent temper which has stalked you since childhood, and being in its grip you inflicted injuries upon Patrick. You may not have killed him directly, but your actions in some fashion resulted in his death.'

'I was nowhere in the vicinity on the night in question, but safe at home with my wife. You can vouch for me can't you, Sarah?'

All eyes were on Sarah. If she confirmed George's alibi, then Isabella's hopes were confounded, but if she refused to endorse his claim, he would be guilty of lying, and much more besides. George was confident she would choose to clear her husband's name rather than adhere strictly to fact.

Through the window Sarah could see the boys crouched on the path with their spinning tops. A thought swooped down on her suddenly, as jinny hoolet upon a field mouse. George still harboured warmth of feeling toward Isabella! He was jealous of the man upon whom Isabella bestowed her affection, to whom she surrendered her heart and body, and it was this serpent of envy, rather than the pursuit of justice, which drove him. The length of Sarah's silence unsettled George. He threw more clods onto the fire, extinguishing the glow and sending thick curls of smoke into the room.

'I cannot vouch for what is not true.' Sarah spoke at last. 'And if I did, Dr Askew would gainsay it. He came that night to treat little Roger's fever and knows George was not at home till gone midnight.'

George saw there was no escape. The Paitson sisters had ambushed him and he must confess, but only what was required to clear him of murder, the rest he still hoped to hide. So George admitted he had indeed met with Patrick that night, and fought with and overcome him, but swore the man was alive and conscious when he left.

They heard Liza call the children from their play. Betty came into the room to draw the curtains and light the lamps and to collect from Sarah the key to the tea caddy and receive instructions regarding which teapot she wished them to use. Sarah waited till Betty was done, then broke the silence.

'What is it you want, Bella? If you insist on pursuing this accusation I will be publicly humiliated, whether George is guilty or no. And your nephews will be ashamed of their father. Would that please you?'

'It would not!' Isabella reached out to take Sarah's hand. 'You are my dear sister and I've no wish to harm you or your sons. I have a proposal to make and, if you accept, I promise to withdraw the charge. I can't raise my child myself, though I am tempted to try, so you must raise it for me. I ask you to treat the child as if it were your own and let it enjoy all the advantages your children enjoy.'

Isabella went on to explain how this might be achieved. Sarah was due to give birth at approximately the same time as she was, George had said as much on their way down to Bolton; when Sarah was brought to bed, Isabella's baby was to be smuggled into Sarah's lying-in chamber and George was to let it be known his wife had given birth to twins. It should not be difficult to find a midwife prepared to keep the secret so long as she was generously recompensed and no one else need ever know the infant's true identity.

Sarah turned the matter over; she bore Isabella no animosity and had no objection to accepting her child, which would not only answer Isabella's predicament but in addition be an ever present humiliation to George, for Sarah was bent on punishing him.

'I accept, on two conditions,' she said at last. 'Firstly the child must be brought up to think I'm its mother, and continue to believe so, as long as I'm alive. The second concerns you, George.' Contempt was etched in the lines around Sarah's mouth as she regarded her husband. 'My mother and sisters will no longer be barred from this house, and no one will prevent them from seeing my children whenever it pleases them. If you consent, then I'll raise Isabella's child. If you refuse, I'll reveal what I know to the High Constable.'

George had no option but to acquiesce and in return the women pledged not to report him. They assured each other that, as George was not directly guilty of murder, nothing would be gained by passing on to the authorities what they knew. Meg took some time to assimilate their reasoning, but at last was convinced and she and Isabella took their leave.

Once in her own home, Isabella was overcome by extreme fatigue. She began to tremble with such severity she could not reply when her mother enquired what ailed her. Her entire body shook, her limbs and her internal organs, heart and lungs and spleen, until she feared the babe in her womb would be shaken loose of its moorings.

Margaret appealed to Mrs Carr who recommended an infusion of hyssop with water purpy, which cured her brother's shaking palsy, and offered to supply two doses of the same, the price to be added to their rent.

George remained in the parlour, brooding, long after the conference was concluded. So, the Paitson sisters had the upper hand and planned to place a cuckoo in his songbird's nest and he must accept it. Had he relayed to Isabella the vulgar manner in which Patrick spoke of her, she might have abandoned her cause. On the other hand, she might have levelled more serious allegations against him. He did well not to take the risk.

Sarah came quietly into the room and settled on the sofa. 'So tell me the truth, George,' she said, without taking her eyes off her needlework. 'What happened that night? '

'When I left, the fellow was on the ground but without serious injury. I've no notion how a man as hale as he, became a corpse floating downstream a few hours later.'

'I'm not asking about that night. I refer to the night you passed with Isabella in the coach house in Bolton. Tell me what really happened.' Sarah continued plying her needle while she waited for his reply.

The crowner examined Patrick's body and discovered injuries to the head, none of a grievous nature, which might indicate a violent encounter of some kind preceding entry to the water, but could just as well be ascribed to buffeting of the body as it was carried downstream. He measured the quantity of water in the stomach and lungs, and concluded the man was alive at the time of immersion; he pronounced drowning the most likely cause of death, although the noxious substances in the water no doubt played their part.

Two witnesses claimed, in their depositions, that they had observed a navvy answering to the description, drinking heavily in the Dyers Arms but could not be sure of the precise hour; another witness testified to hearing an altercation in the vicinity of Miller Bridge, but this evidence was discounted on the grounds its originator was a notorious thief.

The jury duly returned a verdict of death by accident due to an advanced state of inebriation, nevertheless a few continued to favour the notion the unfortunate man had not fallen from the bridge but was pushed.

CHAPTER 19

1800

The weekly visits to Sarah and George's home afforded the Paitson women great delight. Sarah took pride in presenting her sons to their grandmother and aunts, Margaret fed them sugared fruits in paper twists, Meg bounced the little ones in her lap and Isabella played board games with the older boys, ever mindful her child would be raised with them as brothers.

Sarah made no reference to Isabella's condition, lest Liza or Betty overhear, but kept close watch on her sister's general presentation and always sent her home laden with nourishing titbits. George, however, contrived to be absent during their visits.

'And where will you go when the time comes?' Isaac enquired of Isabella one day, embarrassed to be broaching the intimate topic but conscious that Isabella might be in need of assistance.

'The question vexes me and I can't find an answer.' Isabella moved the pile of laundry onto the bed to make space for him to sit. 'It must be somewhere I won't be seen, yet no great distance from here.'

'And somewhere you'll be well cared for,' Isaac added. 'What would you say to Anchorite House? If you approve it, I'll approach them on your behalf.'

'I would say the notion is an excellent one.' Isabella's eyes filled with tears of relief. 'I'll leave the arrangements to you, Isaac. I'm more grateful than I can say.'

Isaac overcame an initial reluctance on the part of the Anchorite spokesman by pledging to make a liberal donation, in addition to defraying the full cost of Isabella's keep, which Isabella insisted she would one day repay. When even the gowns Meg lent her would no longer encompass her waist, Isabella duly informed the guardians of her pupils that she was called away to another part of the country on urgent business and would return only when her responsibilities there were discharged. Next Isabella took her pen and wrote a brief letter.

> George,
> I entrust to your care this infant who is more precious to me than my own life. If it is a boy you are to call him Peter, which as I now know, was the true name of his dear father whose life was ended too early, hastened by your hand. If it is a girl then she will be called Sarah after her adopted mother.
>   I cannot hate you, Georgie, but nor can I forgive what you did. I am watching from my grave and will hold you responsible should any harm befall the child.
> Isabella

She gave the letter to Isaac with instructions that, in the event of her death during childbirth, it was to be delivered to George along with the baby. Isaac reprimanded her for morbid thoughts but accepted the charge nonetheless.

Isabella then took her locking box and went into exile in the hermitage beside the sacred well. To preserve her anonymity, she swathed her body in the voluminous robes worn by the Anchorite servants and drew a veil across her face; there was no danger of her being recognised from the pitch and tone of her voice because the female servants conducted their lives mostly in silence.

In truth her precautions were unnecessary; Kirkby Kendal folk were too busy earning a living and spending what they earned, begetting the next generation and burying the former, sinning and seeking forgiveness for their sins, to care about the disappearance of an unmarried school mistress, approaching the age of forty, who possessed neither wealth nor beauty.

Isabella was comforted by the simplicity of the hermits' life and gladly performed the chores allotted to her, namely sweeping the floor of the servants' quarters and assisting with the serving of meals. However, she kept well away from the poor who lay, sick and dying, in the infirmary, in case she herself fall ill and harm her unborn child. She attended prayers sparingly, only when not to do so would earn a reprimand, for she took no comfort in kneeling with bowed head before an unknown and invisible being to beg forgiveness and seek blessing, when her fellow mortals could grant both and more effectively.

One of the Anchorite servants, known to all as Jennet Jane, took a liking to Isabella. Jane did not reside in the house but came in daily to scrape the milky discharge from the rags used to bind patients' sores, before bleaching the cloths with lime. Her face was hideously pox-scarred and only one solitary tooth remained in her gums; when she spoke her words slipped through the deep cleft in her upper lip.

From time to time, Jane would beckon Isabella to join her in the yard behind the house and there took snuff and declaimed on worldly matters while Isabella provided a silent audience.

'Are you carrying a boy or a girl?' Jane enquired one day. 'Here's how to tell; if the hairs on your legs grow thick and your piss is like gold, then you'll have a boy, and if not then you must make do with a girl.' Though she knew it was nonsense, Isabella examined both and found the answer to the first was no and to the second yes, which left her none the wiser.

'My first time, it was as though a butcher's knife clove my belly in two,' Jennet Jane confided on another occasion. 'I cursed and hollered and thrashed so wildly the midwife was obliged to call my husband and brothers to hold me down!' Isabella listened in dismay.

Every afternoon Isabella rested; lying on her bed she gazed at the sky, which was all that was visible through windows positioned high up in the walls to prevent outsiders peeping in. She noted how the cloud formations frequently mirrored the patterns · found on the earth beneath; the deep ridges left by the plough, the wavy runnels worn by water running over soft soil, and the snow-covered hills rising in the distance.

One afternoon, luxuriating in the lazy realm between sleep and wakefulness, Isabella watched little bundles of white cloud float by, light as the breast feathers of a dove, but with their centres carelessly blocked out in dark charcoal. A sharp pain gripped her innards and she hurried to empty her bowels, but when the spasms continued at intervals throughout the afternoon she guessed the birth must be imminent.

Excited and fearful, Isabella went in search of Jane, who was to attend as midwife, and at last came upon her in the kitchen. Jane left off kneading dough and led Isabella to the room which was to serve as lying-in chamber. Isabella could just make out a small bed pushed against one wall but there was no other furniture.

'Must the window be closed?' Isabella asked. 'I'll suffocate in the absence of fresh air, and the room appears gloomy. I prefer it light and cheering.'

'Well, you may open it if you wish,' said Jane reluctantly. 'But they do say evil spirits enter through open windows, though I'm sure you will call it nonsense.'

Isabella left the window shut; she knew it was mere superstition but at that moment she was not prepared to take any risks. When Jane returned with extra bed linen and bolsters and a basin of water, she found Isabella bent double and grunting as another spasm turned her stomach muscles to iron.

The pain was more severe than any Isabella had previously endured and she did what she could to divert her mind from it, reciting lines of poetry, chanting numbers backwards and singing songs with tuneful refrains. When the next cramp struck Isabella curled up on the bare floor, and for the next she stretched out on the bed.

'Here, take this.' Jane held out a length of polished timber. 'When they are at their worst, place it between your teeth and bite as hard as you dare.' Jane crouched down to work her fingers across Isabella's hips and up and down her spine.

'Is there nothing you can give to deaden the senses?' Isabella gasped.

'You can sup the caudle I brought from home.' Jane held the jug of warm liquid to Isabella's lips.

Isabella was racked with pain hour after hour until her mind turned to wool and her body seemed to float round the room, from time to time colliding with others who floated there too. An irate gentleman with a red beard full of spittle shouted at her, a young woman with huge eyes implored Isabella to have pity. The face of Jennet Jane hovered into view for a moment before dissolving into a muddy pool. Someone tied successive bands of cloth around Isabella's body, forcing the baby downwards but, before she could protest, the bands became Patrick's arms and she drifted off into delirium.

Fearing for the life of mother and child, Jane sent for the apothecary-surgeon stationed in the Anchorite infirmary. He carried out a brief examination and was alarmed at Isabella's condition.

'Why didn't you call me earlier?' he asked sharply. 'The case is dire and the mother may not survive. Remove these bands at once!'

'I called you just as soon as I saw she was in difficulty. She is a woman of strong mind and constitution and there was no reason to suspect complications,' Jane protested. If published abroad, the aspersions he cast on her skill as midwife would leave few willing to call upon her services.

'I suspect you've done more harm than good. There's naught else for it; I must apply forceps,' the surgeon declared. The sound of his voice drifted down to Isabella as though from a great distance and she demanded to know which man it was that dared come near at such a time.

'Thank the Lord she's with us yet!' Jane murmured. 'Hold my hand as tight as you wish, my dear. The surgeon here will have that troublesome one out in no time.'

After a few attempts, the apothecary surgeon succeeded in grasping the baby's head and, with the next spasm, drew it from the shelter of its mother's body, to Isabella's indescribable relief. Within the hour she was sufficiently revived to have her son snuggly by her side and to feel the flutter of his new-born heart against her chest. When they tried to take him from her, Isabella refused to surrender him.

'You only store up greater sorrow for yourself by growing fond of the wee hapless thing,' said Jennet Jane, tutting toothlessly.

'It's a price I'm happy to pay,' Isabella tightened her hold on the baby. For five precious days she kept him by her side and watched in adoration while he suckled and slept and suckled again. Sometimes she hummed lullabies or whispered children's rhymes, but mostly she lay in silence, her arms encircling the pulsing warmth of him as they had once encircled his father.

Meanwhile, at the other end of the town, George waited until Sarah's pains followed one upon another in quick succession, then set out for Anchorite House to collect the bastard who in future must count as his own child. Hearing news of George's arrival, Isabella wrapped her son in a shawl of fine bobbin lace and laid him in the centre of the bed. Then she removed herself to the far corner of the chamber, her forehead pressed against the roughness of the wall, so she might not see the hands which bore away this symbol of her love for Patrick, and her forefingers pressed into her ears, lest the sound of his whimpers and snuffles break her resolve.

While Isabella's back was turned, Jane lifted the baby boy and deftly wound a plain sheet round him then administered a little black drop in his pink mouth so that, when she handed the bundle to George, there were no cries. George placed the bundle in a basket and carried it for all the world as though he were returning from market with a chyne of lamb. On arriving home he was met by the midwife attending to Sarah. She took the basket from him.

'Your wife is delivered of a baby girl,' she whispered. 'A sickly thing and grotesque; its chest palpitates rapidly in the manner of a fish drawn from water. It won't live beyond a few hours. Mrs Moser knows nothing of this misfortune; I thought it best to consult you before telling her.'

George entered Sarah's chamber to see for himself. The little girl was indeed unpleasant to behold, her skull was misshapen and one arm turned back on itself. George felt a mixture of revulsion and pity.

'She's to be called Dorothy,' Sarah announced. 'I can scarce believe it! A daughter after so many sons. Bring her to me, I've yet to see her face.' Sarah's smile vanished on seeing George's expression. 'What is it? Is something wrong with the child?'

The curate made all possible haste, but Dorothy passed away before she was absolved from sin. Fortunately the doctor who attended later was so intrigued by the deformity, a version of headmouldshot not referred to in the textbooks, he omitted to examine the other twin; had he done so he would have been perplexed to discover a boy already a few days old.

'Take this little one.' The midwife placed Isabella's son in Sarah's arms. 'He's as much in need of a mother's care, as you're in need of a baby to cherish.'

'I won't hold another's offspring when I can't hold my own.' Sarah pushed the baby aside without so much as looking at him.

'At least let him suckle.' The midwife proffered the infant once more. 'He's denied his mother's milk while you have milk to spare.'

'If Dorothy can't drink my milk, then no babe shall.' Sarah folded her arms and turned her dull eyes inwards.

With nothing to stimulate the flow, her milk soon dried up while, at Anchorite House, Isabella applied poultices to reduce the inflammation in her overflowing breasts.

CHAPTER 20

1800

Isabella was welcomed home by Mrs Carr who exhibited remarkable self-censorship and refrained from delving into the reasons for her lodger's absence. The guardians of Isabella's pupils, too, were content to curb their curiosity and return their children to her care, for had not Miss Paitson proved her worth as schoolmistress? Isabella opened the classroom doors and resumed lessons immediately, but her thoughts were directed to the visit she planned to make that afternoon.

'Describe his appearance to me, Mamma.' Isabella walked slowly towards George and Sarah's residence, her mother leaning on her arm. 'Does Sarah cherish him like her own son, and how do his brothers receive him?'

'He resembles your father most closely.' Margaret smiled at her daughter's childlike eagerness. 'His hair grows low on his forehead and his jaw promises to be strong once the bones are fully formed. Whether he'll be blessed with the same temperament as his grandfather, it's too early to say.' Here Margaret paused to catch her breath. 'But you must understand this, Sarah exhibits the symptoms of melancholia. Dr Askew prescribes bed rest and a little laudanum, which leaves her unfit to attend to any aspect of the household or indeed care for her own children. The baby is largely given into Betty's charge, which is for the best as Betty dotes on him.'

Isabella was disturbed by this news; if Peter was assigned to the care of servants he would acquire their speech and manners. How then would he hold his own later in life?

'You make excuses for them!' she said. 'Sarah and George insult Peter and go against our agreement.'

'It's to be expected, considering the circumstances.' Margaret did not share Isabella's modern views. 'You would do well to be grateful, Bella. Peter's fortunes could have been far worse. Remember, Sarah's daughter lies underground, while your son lives.'

Isabella berated herself for not bearing this in mind; the mere contemplation of harm befalling Peter set her heart pounding and blocked her breath.

When they arrived at the house, Isabella went straight to Sarah's room and was shocked to see her sister lying on her four-poster, dull eyed and gaunt. Her hands were mere bone and wrinkled skin, like the feet of fowl, her auburn hair was streaked with white and her figure shrunk to a mockery of its former fullness.

'It was the two events together, you understand, Bella.' Sarah's voice was weak. 'To discover my husband never cared for me and to give birth to a monster in place of a daughter. The one I might have borne, comforted by the other, but to lose both at once has done for me.'

'You haven't lost your husband! George prays for your speedy recovery as do we all. And the boys ask after you continually.' Isabella rubbed Sarah's cold, limp hands.

'You don't need to defend him. I know what George did, or at least what he attempted. He cared only for you from the beginning, Bella, and made a mockery of our marriage. Now he despises me as I despise him.' Sarah had deduced for herself what happened in Bolton, and the knowledge banished forever the contented wife and mother she had been, prior to acquiring it.

'You're mistaken. George had no thoughts of me these ten years.' Isabella went to draw back the curtains. 'He merely availed himself of an opportunity, and at a time when his judgement was distorted by strong drink.'

'Remember how I complained my beauty would be spoilt by starvation? It's grief, not want of nourishment, has killed it.' Sarah picked up the giltwood looking-glass her father bequeathed her and gazed in disgust at her own image.

'Your beauty isn't lost but only hidden beneath your sorrow and will soon return.' Isabella took the mirror and placed it out of reach.

She sat an hour beside the bed but throughout that time Sarah made no mention of Peter, and when Isabella asked to see the new addition to the family, Sarah showed no interest. It was Betty who conducted Isabella into the rear chamber where baby Peter lay sleeping. Isabella longed to cradle him in her arms but dare not for fear Betty would be suspicious. Instead she ran her fingertips lightly over Peter's unblemished cheek and caressed the fragile curve of his tiny head.

Isaac called on Isabella that evening, on his way back from the Bowling Green, to hear how the visit went.

'Peter is wrapped in a torn cloth which is none too clean,' Isabella complained. 'He sleeps in an old drawer when I know the other boys slept in a cradle made of sweet apple wood. He's treated less favourably than his brothers. You must have noticed it yourself.'

'I dare say things will improve when Sarah is restored to soundness of mind.' Isaac sought to avert his eyes from the heap of women's garments beside him, waiting to be laundered. 'My advice is to be patient. You would only make matters worse by protesting and Peter is in no danger.'

'I won't stand by and watch my son neglected. If he can't have their love, he must at least have their respect.' Isabella was suddenly assailed by doubts. Since giving birth she seemed often to waver and hesitate, where before she adhered to her determined path. 'Perhaps I was wrong to give him away and would have done better to raise him myself?'

'You gave him away for good reason. Before long Sarah will rally and matters will improve.' Isaac spoke more in hope than certainty.

And indeed Isaac's prediction proved only partially

correct; Sarah rallied but there was no improvement in Peter's lot. Visiting one evening, Isabella was vexed to see the children at table while Peter ate his meal in the kitchen. On another occasion the other boys gathered round their mother while she set them riddles, but Peter was not amongst their number; upon investigation Isabella found him playing in the dirt while Liza scoured the cooking pots in the yard.

Isabella was familiar with the views espoused in *A Vindication* in regard to parental affection, and concurred with their condemnation of the "brutal love" displayed by mothers who promoted the advancement of their children at all costs. However, she considered her case to be different; she was responsible for Peter's disadvantages and therefore felt entitled to do all she could to secure the right conditions for his upbringing. So, when she saw her appeals to Sarah had no effect, Isabella sought an audience with George.

'I don't believe your sister neglects him willfully.' George was nursing a gout-ridden leg which made him more than usually irritable. 'Peter is the age Dorothy would have been; each time Sarah encounters your son she's reminded of the daughter of whom she was cheated. It's natural she keeps him at a distance. We've taken him into our home, what more can you expect?'

'I can expect you to do all that's needful to prevent the authorities hearing the truth about your conduct around the time a certain individual's body was found in the river.' Isabella spoke slowly so her drift could not be mistaken. 'I expect my son to be regarded in every respect as your own.'

1803

When Margaret passed away at the grand age of seventy plus seven, Isabella felt the loss keenly. She had slept under the same roof as her mother every night for the past forty-two years, save the few weeks she spent with the Anchorites. Margaret faced death with equanimity sustained by the simple faith that if she had lived her life well she would be rewarded; no one could doubt she was now with her Maker.

Isaac understood the emptiness Isabella experienced, his father, Joseph, having died but a few months earlier. Isaac developed the habit of calling on Isabella most days, accompanying her on errands and, as neither enjoyed dining alone, often shared a meal with her to their mutual comfort. Conversation flowed more readily between them than formally, which Isaac found gratifying for he was in general a man of few words, especially in the presence of ladies.

One day they were making purchases from a shop in Stramongate and deliberating which was preferable, the tortoiseshell comb or the comb carved from bone, when Betty appeared unexpectedly in the doorway, quite out of breath and weeping.

'Miss Isabella, come quickly, I beg you!' she gasped. 'They found him in the warehouse this morning and sent at once for Dr Askew and the mistress is beside herself and the poor children don't know what to make of it.'

'Who did they find in the warehouse? Calm yourself, Betty, and tell me who it was they found.' Isabella's purse dropped to the floor.

'The master. Though you'd hardly recognise him, his face all bloodied and discoloured,' Betty said between sobs. 'The mistress is wailing something terrible at being left a widow with five sons to raise, and will not heed those who try to calm her.'

'I must go to Sarah right away,' Isabella said. 'Betty, you go to Mrs Pooley and tell her what you've told me and ask her to come immediately.'

'It's best if you take Betty with you, Isabella.' Isaac bent to retrieve the spilled coins. 'I'll fetch Meg and we'll join you later.'

Isabella was assailed by a multitude of emotions as she and Betty hurried to the Moser residence; shock at the news of George's death and regret he should die a stranger to her affections; fear for Sarah's sanity as this second blow came while she was not yet recovered from her previous loss; and a deep anxiety about the treatment Peter would receive now his champion and protector was no more. In spite of everything, Isabella must maintain her composure; how else would she provide comfort to the bereaved?

They arrived to find Sarah standing in the centre of the kitchen, unshod and clad only in a chemise. She demanded Liza fetch her a phial of white arsenic so she could swallow it and escape her cursed existence; to which Liza replied she would do no such thing, and did Sarah not know better than to take on so in front of the children? The boys themselves stood against the wall, looking in bewilderment at their mother and Liza, unable to comprehend the scene.

'What's this, Sarah? Already mid-morning and you haven't finished dressing!' Isabella adopted a firm tone. 'We're expecting guests to arrive within the hour. You wouldn't wish to appear before guests in this condition, would you?'

'Guests? I've invited no one.' Sarah fingered her chemise and put a hand to her uncombed hair.

'But folk will come uninvited when they hear the news. And you must greet them and thank them for their trouble.' Isabella led the way upstairs, and Sarah did not resist.

In due course Isaac's carriage drew up and Meg disembarked along with her box. She insisted on taking charge of the running of the household, indeed she was glad of the diversion, for her house was dismal bereft of Mr Pooley and she was dismal within it. Meg wasted no time and went immediately to the kitchen to consult with

Betty and inspect the state of the larder.

Meanwhile Isabella undertook to come each day to attend to the children who were sorely in need of comfort. She embraced them if they were tearful and answered their questions with infinite patience, and at night stayed in their room until they were sleeping deeply. But she kissed her own son a little more tenderly, and lingered a little longer at his bedside. Betty and Liza noticed the favouritism, but thought nothing of it, attributing the preferential treatment to Peter being the youngest.

Isabella was pleased to discover Peter was blessed with a cheerful disposition; he woke with a smile and contentment was his companion throughout the day. If he fell and hurt himself he was more likely to laugh than cry; he did not grizzle when woken from a nap and never complained when his brothers snatched playthings from his grasp.

His easy-going attitude would no doubt earn him popularity but would not be conducive to making his way in life. Book learning, for instance, required concentration and perseverance, traits Peter had yet to display; he was already capable of tracing letters on a slate but, when Isabella gave him the chalk, he ran off laughing. Isabella suspected he inherited these aspects of his character from Patrick and was confident the fault could be rectified with discipline. Oh, how she wished she had charge of Peter's upbringing.

Dr Askew examined George's corpse and reported it was livergrown from frequent and excessive recourse to strong drink. He named a blow to the head as immediate cause of death, most probably incurred as the result of a fall, and was of the opinion the fall itself was due to weakness in the left leg where mortification extended from foot to knee.

'I warned Mr Moser, only last week.' Dr Askew sat taking tea with Isaac. 'The poison threatens to spread throughout the body and on that account the leg must be removed. The decision was not an easy one. Mr Moser proposed to seek advice, I believe.'

'George rarely asked advice upon any matter.' Isaac passed his snuff box to the good doctor. 'And if given unsolicited, he refused to heed it.'

The parish church boasted a peal of eight weighty bells, but only one tolled the morning of George's funeral. Roger Moser supplied his family and servants with best quality mourning, and sent carriages for the most honoured guests; led by the hearse, the procession travelled sedately from the home of the deceased towards the parish church where a crowd gathered to watch as the vicar guided the pall-bearers inside.

The service itself was attended by a large congregation including a number of worthy dignitaries, and was conducted with pomp, since George Moser was a man of some repute. The vicar preached a long and sombre sermon taking for his text the First Epistle to Timothy, chapter six, verses seven, eight and nine, which struck Isabella as uncomfortably close to the mark:

> For we brought nothing into this world, and it is certain we can carry nothing out. And having food and raiment let us be therewith content. But they that will be rich fall into temptation and a snare, and into many foolish and hurtful lusts, which drown men, in destruction and perdition.

Afterwards Isabella and Isaac joined Roger and Elizabeth Moser without the church, greeting the mourners and accepting condolences on behalf of the deceased's widow, Sarah herself being too distraught to attend, and inviting them to partake of toast and cake and wine if they were so inclined.

'A sad business, to leave so many sons fatherless,' Capstick remarked as he shook Isaac's hand. 'George Moser deserved better; he was a man of his word and a shrewd businessman.'

'And generous to the poor and needy,' added Samuel Shaw, stabbing his walking stick into the ground to augment his praise. 'I've seen Mr Moser wipe out what was due to him when upright and deserving men in his employ were at their wits' end how to pay.'

'That may be true, but you can't deny his hot temper.' Samuel's wife linked her arm through his. 'I've seen him strike out in anger when he should have known better. Something gnawed at him but I'm at a loss to say what it was.'

That night Isabella took out her little bible in search of three locks of hair placed there more than thirty years earlier; there was no doubt, their friendship in those days was deep and genuine, if only it could have been preserved. She thought sadly of the gradual change in George from young lad, warm and spontaneous and often up to mischief, to dealer in cloth with the fixed intention of making Isabella his wife whether she willed it or no, to the man so poisoned by jealousy and desire for vengeance he caused the death of another.

Isabella continued idly turning the pages of the little book. Part way through the Song of Solomon she was arrested by the sight of letters scribbled close to the spine; "I.P. & P.F." Had she really written that? How absurd! How childish! In spite of her embarrassment, the exhilaration of those weeks with Patrick coursed Isabella's veins, an insubstantial echo of the true emotions, but enough to warm her cheeks.

The sensation forced Isabella to acknowledge how much she too had changed; once an innocent, sweet-natured girl dreaming of true love, she became the woman who stubbornly desired, and gave herself to, a man most would consider unsuitable, and then, as a consequence, became a mother prepared to resort to blackmail to protect her child.

Only Isaac remained unaltered in every aspect, even down to his appearance; he did not develop the paunch and double chin most men acquire with advancing age. When she was young, Isabella found Isaac's lack of aspiration and conservative outlook dull; now she applauded his even-temper and consistency and counted herself fortunate to have his example ever before her.

Meanwhile, in his own house a little further down the street, Isaac paced the floor with hands clasped behind his back, and turned over in his mind an important matter. He went out into the yard and stood a while, arms now folded across his chest; he studied the half-formed moon with its wispy halo, then returned to the house and continued pacing. Finally he summoned Martha.

'May I put a case to you, Martha, on behalf of a friend?' Martha nodded her agreement. 'My friend is a bachelor approaching his fortieth year and has for the best part of his life been closely acquainted with a spinster of the same age; neither is spoken for, you understand, nor has any prospects of matrimony.' Isaac indicated Martha should sit opposite him.

'These two have been friends a long while, as I say,' he continued, 'and have never thought or spoken of being anything other. Now, my friend has of late begun to experience bouts of acute loneliness and wishes to share his home with a companion.'

'I'm with you so far, sir.' Martha understood the direction of his argument but feigned ignorance.

'Now, you're a woman, so tell me this. How would the aforementioned spinster receive it, if my friend were to raise the question of matrimony? Remember, till now there has never been any suggestion of such an arrangement. Will she take offence and break off their association, an eventuality my friend wishes to avoid at all costs, or will she welcome his proposal?' Isaac left the table and resumed pacing, his hands now locked together and placed on top of his head.

'Well sir, it depends on the circumstances of the lady in question, and on what your friend has to offer.' Martha delivered her answer with a seriousness she hoped would deceive.

'Offer? You mean property and wealth?' Isaac came and sat opposite Martha once more. 'There my friend has the advantage; the lady has limited means and would assuredly benefit from becoming his wife, but I can't be certain, I mean my friend can't be certain, that the woman accords any significance to the question of wealth. He suspects emotion and integrity are uppermost in her mind.'

'Then I can't help you,' Martha said firmly. 'I can't conceive of a woman who wouldn't choose to live in a house like this rather than in rented rooms in a lodging house.'

'I made no mention of a lodging house.' Isaac looked at Martha in alarm.

'It's no use pretending, sir. I know you speak of yourself.' Martha's broad smile revealed near-toothless gums. 'My advice would be to go ahead and put the question, and my guess is Miss Paitson will give you a favourable reply.'

And Martha was right; Isabella took but twenty-four hours to consider before accepting. Isaac obtained a marriage bond and within the week they were wed. Isabella wore a woollen cloak over her simple gown, it being the month of November, and walked up the aisle without bridesmaids. Afterwards, the guests were served a glass of wine, with small beer for the children, and a collation of cold meats prepared by Meg.

'Are you contented, my dear?' Isaac took Isabella's

hand as they sat side by side, reviewing the day's proceedings after the last guest had departed. 'Speaking for myself I don't believe it's possible for anyone to be happier.'

'Overjoyed describes my sentiments more accurately. But, yes, contented also,' Isabella said, looking into the glowing embers. 'However there is one thing which would make my happiness complete.'

'Does it concern Peter?'

'It does.' Isabella smiled gratefully at her husband. 'The child has a tendency to idleness which can be corrected but I doubt Sarah has either the energy or the enthusiasm for it. If Peter lived here with us, I could see to it this weakness was overcome.'

'But how would you explain the transfer without arousing suspicion?' Isaac pondered the matter a while. 'Unless we were to host two of the boys, say John in addition to Peter, while the three older boys remained with their mother, then it would appear we simply sought to share the load.' Isaac did not relish the thought of adding two young boys to his household, but was willing to do so for the sake of Isabella's peace of mind.

'What an excellent idea! I think I can persuade Sarah, but it will take longer to convince Elizabeth Moser to allow two of her grandsons to remain in my house. She has never forgiven me for rejecting and humiliating her only son.'

They agreed Isabella would put the suggestion to Sarah the next morning, while Isaac called on Roger and Elizabeth to recommend the plan to them and outline its advantages.

CHAPTER 21

1827

Isabella and Peter stood on the east bank of the River Kent, at the point where it looped and divided to form an island. Here stood an elegant row of dwelling houses three stories high, recently erected and known as Kent Terrace. The buildings were constructed of limestone ashlar, cut and polished to unparalleled smoothness and inside the rooms were well-proportioned and spacious.

Peter planned to lay down a deposit on one of the properties, using for capital the legacy he received on his mother's recent demise, a sum equal to that received by his brothers as stipulated in George Moser's will. Isabella was present to give her opinion on the investment; it was also her intention to divulge the secret which had lain heavy on her these past twenty seven years.

'I own the situation is salubrious being at a little distance from the town.' Isabella regarded the facades doubtfully. 'And the houses are built to a handsome design, indeed rather too handsome for a young attorney, not yet established. Wouldn't it be prudent to settle for something a little less grand?'

'Before you form an opinion, Aunt Isabella, have a look at the view which will greet me on waking, and see if that doesn't convince you.' Peter placed his hands lightly on Isabella's shoulders and spun her round to face in the opposite direction, as he had spun her round throughout his childhood, with his innocent look and charming smile, so that she could never bear to scold or punish him for more than a few minutes, despite her best intentions.

'There now, what do you say to that?' Peter's eyes shone with pride as though the property was already his.

The view was indeed pretty; tumbling crests chased each other downstream towards the three arches of Miller Bridge. Livestock grazed beside the rows of tenters running across Gooseholme, and children played at the water's edge while their mothers laid out food for a picnic; men with fishing rods dotted the banks, and families strolled along the river path to take the air. Sunlight played over the water, picked out the whiteness of the houses and brightened the blue of the sky. On the far side of the river, the town stretched out before the eye until the land swept upwards to woods and hills and the distinctive crest of Kendal Fell.

'You can walk here at any time and gaze on the view,' Isabella reasoned. 'You don't have to take up residence in one of these houses to enjoy it. I say the price is beyond your reach.'

Peter was often absent from his desk at J&P Moser, and therefore drew a lesser sum than John who worked a full day and was remunerated correspondingly. This had always been the way; as boys John applied himself earnestly to his studies while Peter expended the least energy required to get by, then went off in pursuit of entertainment.

Isaac's nephew, Edward, who had taken the brothers on as trainee attorneys, could scarce believe the two were brothers, so different were their attitudes. He did not know how true his observation.

'Uncle Thompson matched John pound for pound when he contracted for his mortgage.' Peter put a persuasive arm round Isabella. 'I have no doubt Uncle will do likewise for me.'

'That was because John needed somewhere to accommodate his wife and child; your case is different.' Isabella gently chaffed the hand resting on her shoulder. 'Unless you're about to make an announcement, which I think unlikely. I've noticed you prefer to keep company with many different women than to restrict yourself to one!'

'John is too serious and has never known how to enjoy

life. To that extent he takes after the Paitson sisters.' Peter pulled down the corners of his mouth. 'Was my father so sombre? I think not. I suspect I inherit from him my reluctance to view any matter too seriously. Isn't that the case, Aunt Isabella?'

Isabella dismissed the question with a smile. But as they walked home arm in arm, she told Peter she wished to speak to him on a delicate but weighty matter which he might find unpalatable.

'You ask if your nature is patterned on that of George Moser; the question is meaningless because he was not your father.' Isabella watched Peter's expression anxiously. 'There is no Moser blood flowing in your veins.'

'Then did my mother ...?' Peter halted and stared at Isabella in disbelief.

'No, no! Sarah did not behave improperly.'

'How is that possible...?' Peter looked bewildered.

'The truth is, Sarah was not your mother either. I wasn't at liberty to tell you so until after her death, but now she is no longer with us I can't keep it to myself.'

'Not my mother! And her husband not my father! What is it you wish to tell me, Aunt Isabella? Am I some wretched orphan left at the Workhouse door, or the son of a prince fallen on hard times?' Peter chose to make light of what he heard; to take Isabella's statements seriously would be to destroy everything he knew about his lineage.

'I'm the woman who gave birth to you, Peter. I'm your mother though you've been raised to think of me as aunt. I would have told you earlier but I gave my word.'

Isabella told him as much of the story as he needed to know; she took care to present Patrick in as favourable a manner as possible and to omit anything that tarnished his or George's good character, but she could do nothing to obscure the part she played and knew she exposed herself to condemnation.

When the tale was concluded, Isabella dared not look

at her son's face to learn how he received it. Peter continued in silence some while, then asked whether it had not occurred to Isabella he might prefer to remain in ignorance.

'I confess it did not,' she said. 'I was bent on sharing my secret and didn't consider your feelings. Is it a great disappointment to learn I'm your mother?'

'No! It's a shock, but not a disappointment. You've been my mother, to all intents and purposes, and I couldn't ask for better. But it will take time to grow used to the idea.'

Peter walked on ahead, preoccupied with his own musings. It was unsettling to know so little of Patrick but, as he had no memories of George Moser either, the matter did not disturb him overmuch. No, it was the notion of Aunt Isabella conducting a clandestine affair which shook him. A little earlier he had berated the Paitson sisters for their sober attitude to life, a judgement he now understood to be false, at least so far as Isabella was concerned. She reached out and took her chance of happiness, knowing the liaison would never be publicly endorsed. In some respects Peter disapproved of Isabella's impropriety, yet in his heart he also admired her for it.

The sun was warm upon his back and the air balmy; he had no wish to waste such a day sitting behind a desk and, in any case, it would be unwise to return to the office. Despite the differences in their characters, he and John understood each other's thoughts before they were uttered and John would sense immediately that something of significance had occurred.

Peter walked on, careless of the direction he took, until he found himself ascending Serpentine Walk, a path across the fells and through woodland laid down a few years ago at the expense of local benefactors. Peter rarely spent any time alone, preferring to be diverted by the company of others, and it was therefore not his custom to observe any scene in depth. Today, however, he took careful note of his surroundings.

The hogweed rose stiffly to tower above tall graceful grasses, and lower down nettles dangled their strings of tiny seeds like pale green chandeliers; the gold of buttercups poked boldly through the undergrowth, and the creamy clusters of elderflowers and the white blossom of bramble and musk rose were scattered everywhere.

Peter wished he were free to speak openly to John regarding Aunt Isabella's disclosure; as boys, he and John believed their mother chose to give them up because she cared more for their older brothers. John would be relieved to know this was not the case.

Butterflies and bees flew from flower to flower and wood pigeons pecked the fruits of the wild cherry. Peter reached up and picked some of the fruits, staining his gloves scarlet, and popped them in his mouth where they released their juiciness in sudden bursts.

On his return home, Peter found John's carriage pulled up before the door and heard his sister-in-law conversing with Isaac and Isabella; he heard another voice also, a woman's tones, clear and resonant as the striking of the small clock, yet as rich as the clarinet and more refined in accent than the speech of Kirkby Kendal folk. Eager to meet the owner of this voice, Peter went straight to the parlour.

'Peter! We were speaking of you just this minute.' John's wife rose from her chair and looked at him with evident affection. 'I feared we might be obliged to leave without seeing you. Let me introduce my cousin, arrived this day from Colchester. Mary Elizabeth, this is my husband's younger brother.'

'It is a pleasure to meet you, Peter. I was just complimenting your uncle and aunt on the majesty of the hills I passed through on the journey here.'

Mary Elizabeth extended her hand and Peter found

himself looking into the bluest of blue eyes, bordered by the longest of lashes; ringlets of deep gold hung down on each side of Mary Elizabeth's sweet face while the remaining tresses were gathered loosely into a bun and the whole topped with an apple-green bonnet.

'The pleasure is all mine.' Peter's eyes ran over the short, tightfitting spencer jacket, the delicately smocked gown with a low waist which enhanced her slender figure, and the silk parasol resting gracefully in one hand. 'I'm glad I arrived before you left. No, I'm more than glad, I'm delighted! You must let me show you round. We'll begin with the Castle. We'll take a picnic; Aunt Isabella is excellent at picnics! Do say you'll come.' He knew he grinned absurdly but was powerless to stop.

Mary Elizabeth thanked him for the invitation, which she accepted, and the two of them spent the next half hour happily comparing the castles and climates of Colchester and Kirkby Kendal, and boasting of canals and corn exchanges; all of which left Peter in no doubt that Mary Elizabeth possessed a good brain in addition to beauty. When he retired that night, Peter dreamt of a palace constructed of limestone ashlar, floating down the River Kent supported by four swans with golden feathers and eyes of the most brilliant blue.

The following morning, Isabella asked Peter to wait a few moments before setting off for the office of J&P Moser as she had something to give him.

'I'd like you to have this.' She held out a little bible snug within its own pouch. 'My mother gave it me over fifty years ago. I doubt you'll have much use for it at present, though as you grow older you may find some passages speak to your condition. Keep it safe and pass it on to your own son or daughter.'

Peter thanked her and slipped the little book into his bag along with his papers. It was not till late afternoon that he remembered and took it out to have a proper look. He noted the tooled leather work inlaid with gold, then flipped through the pages which were densely covered in the smallest print he had ever seen. Returning to the first page, Peter came face to face with Isabella's inscription; he would follow her example and record the transference of ownership.

He dipped his pen and was about to write "Peter Moser's Book" when it occurred to him Peter Paitson or Peter Flanagan would be nearer the truth for, as Isabella pointed out, not a drop of Moser blood flowed through his veins. Well, he could not alter his signature and Peter Moser must suffice. However he could devise a form of words which included both Isabella's maiden and married names, for through her he was indeed a Paitson, and no one could have been a better father to him than Isaac Thompson. He settled upon "Isabella Thompson, late Paitson" and was satisfied.

As he applied the blotter Peter noted one blank page remained. One day his son would write his name as proudly as his father and grandmother had done. Peter already had some idea of what that child might look like.

CHAPTER 22

2007

'I've never been to Kendal.' Tibby struggled with the seat belt. The arthritis in her hands was painful that morning. 'But I've tasted Kendal mint cake. Years ago. One of the admin staff brought some back after her holiday. I liked the brown better than the white.'

'I've heard of Kendal green,' Lottie said. 'The colour I mean. I'm sure it comes in Shakespeare.' She adjusted the mirror then handed Tibby the road atlas, not that there was any chance of getting lost. They might need it in an emergency, though, if they wanted to follow a different route to avoid roadworks or an accident.

Tibby dozed off as soon as they got underway. She looked much older asleep, her head lolling to one side and mouth hanging open, her bright expression replaced by a slack-cheeked vulnerability.

Lottie usually relied on conversation to keep her alert on long journeys. She didn't want to turn on the radio, in case it disturbed Tibby, so instead she played mental games with car registration plates, working her way through the alphabet first then numbers. Tibby resurfaced when the pace slowed as they approached Manchester and crawled through the congestion.

'How long would this journey have taken in Isabella's lifetime?' Lottie asked.

'A few days probably.' Tibby yawned. 'She'd have to stay overnight at coaching stations. Think how long it would take for a letter to arrive. And no telephones.'

They stopped briefly for toilets and coffee. The traffic lightened as they drove further north through ever more beautiful scenery until at last they left the dual carriageway and dropped down into the town of Kendal. The place struck Tibby at first sight as somewhat depressing with its row upon row of grey slate buildings and dull, damp atmosphere not to mention the confusing one-way system.

It began to drizzle, fortunately they were both equipped with umbrellas. They started with the Parish Church, an unnaturally wide building squatting like a toad on the riverbank. Inside it was surprisingly light and airy and wholesome, without any of the sense of mystery Tibby associated with old churches, though the floors and ceilings were scattered with ancient memorials.

She went outside and spent a while reading the gravestones before she found what she was looking for. She brushed the surface clear of leaves and scraped off some of the moss so that Lottie could take photographs of the grave of Andrew Paitson, his wife Margaret and daughter Agnes. It was strangely moving to see the actual burial place of people who, up till then, lived only in her imagination.

They set off towards the centre of town. It wasn't too difficult to shut out the shops and tourists and traffic and pretend they were in the eighteenth century. Lottie put on an imaginary mantua with hooped petticoat, and tied a bonnet over her piled up hair; Tibby chose to be Lottie's male escort so she donned imaginary silk stockings, knee breeches and a curly wig.

They walked slowly over the cobbles, no doubt annoying others using the pavement. They studied the houses, each one different from its neighbour and many of them looking as though they survived from Isabella's time. Not in the least dull and depressing as Tibby at first thought. Particularly interesting were the Kendal yards, little clusters of houses, each with its own character and accessed via openings cut through from the main street.

'I can just imagine Isabella peeping through this archway.' Tibby paused to look through an especially narrow entrance.

'Her mother tells her the yards are not nice places for

little girls.' Lottie hurried past with eyes averted in imitation of a little girl.

'But that just makes Isabella more determined to go and see for herself!' Tibby stepped rebelliously into the narrow opening.

Many of the yards boasted plaques describing their former function, in fact the whole town was well supplied with information boards for visitors. From them Tibby learnt Isabella was around to see the Lancaster Canal reach Kendal but died before the opening of the Kendal to Windermere branch railway line. And that the first banks opened in 1788, in time for George Moser, Peter's father, and then folded during the financial crisis of the early 1800s. *Plus la change!* Only today the banks were nationalized rather than being left to collapse.

They queued a long while for lunch as the rain sent tourists scuttling for shelter. Two waiters in black tee shirts hurried from table to table calling to one another in what sounded like an East European language while the queue continued to grow. Once seated Tibby and Lottie took off their wet jackets and ordered the homemade soup with crusty rolls for starters to warm themselves before the salads.

'Some of these people might be related to Isabella.' Lottie waved her fork in a vague circle. 'Couldn't you put an advert in the local paper saying you want to get in touch with her descendants?'

'She didn't have any direct descendants. Nor did Peter, remember? His daughter died of galloping consumption when she was only twenty-one.'

'Okay. But there must be some Mosers or Paitsons who have heard of Isabella or Peter,' Lottie persisted. 'Wouldn't you like to show them the bible?'

'No. I know what would happen. I'd end up feeling guilty and give it to one of them.' Tibby spread butter on the hot roll and watched it melt.

'You rescued it, you have the right to keep it.' A waitress with dyed blonde hair strained back into a little tuft of a ponytail, wheeled a complaining trolley across the room and out into the kitchen. 'Aren't you going to eat that?' Lottie helped herself to the untouched portion of coleslaw on Tibby's plate.

They decided against desert and ordered coffee which came with chocolate mints.

'You're not going to try to trace your father, are you?' Lottie said.

'If he was interested he'd have made some effort to get in touch.' Tibby dabbed at her mouth with a serviette. 'I'm happy with the family I have. I don't need anyone else.' She detected a hint of relief in Lottie's eyes.

They walked down the main street towards St Thomas's church, at the other end of town from Holy Trinity. The pavements here were less crowded and the houses were smaller and quite plain.

'I think it's stopped raining.' Tibby checked the surface of puddles in the tarmac and peered into the clouds.

'Are you sure? I'm not risking frizz.' Lottie stuck out her head experimentally, holding her umbrella to one side then flapping it dry like a fledgling preparing for the maiden flight.

The woman on duty at St Thomas consulted her list of burials then came outside to point out Peter and his wife Mary Elizabeth's gravestone lying flat and half hidden by wet grass. Tibby found the omission of their daughter's name unsettling. She died at the age of twenty-one, why wasn't she buried in her father's grave?

They could find no sign of John Moser's tombstone which seemed strange for such a public figure; he was churchwarden and Mayor at one time. The ever helpful attendant directed them to a series of plaques on the nave wall, one of which commemorated three of John's children who died aged eleven months, six years and thirteen years. A stark reminder that John too had his share of sorrow. For some reason the death of John's children reminded Tibby of the little girl who was still missing in Portugal.

'It's always upsetting to hear of children dying,' the attendant said. 'Especially when their parents are your ancestors.' She laid a sympathetic hand on Tibby's shoulder.

'Thank you,' said Tibby. 'You've been really helpful. We're going to look in the archives now.' She moved off quickly before Lottie could elaborate.

They crossed the road and climbed the steps of County Hall, a standalone building of dignified proportions, then followed the arrows downstairs to the basement where the archives were housed. The woman behind the desk checked Tibby's ID and, using gestures rather than words, guided her through the document request form. Lottie settled herself amongst a number of people staring earnestly at computer screens and microfiche viewers. Two young women exchanged occasional whispers in American accents. While she waited, Lottie attended to a broken nail.

Tibby went over to look more carefully at the series of maps displayed on the wall. Maps had always fascinated her. As a small child she drew maps in which each house had a door knob, patterned curtains, and occupants lying flat on their backs in a row. Then, when she was in her teens, she would walk through her home town taking the first right and first left, or second right and second left, then reverse the pattern on the way back. As soon as she arrived home she would take out the A to Z and see if she could trace the route she'd taken.

A map of Kendal produced in the 1780s caught her eye. It showed north-south streets lying horizontally and each house had its own ornamental garden full of shrubs, complete with individual shadows. Neatly drawn tenters for drying cloth were lined up on the outskirts of town and inset cameos depicted the town's principal buildings.

There were no tenters in the 1833 map but many of the houses were labelled with their owner's name. Tibby found Kent Terrace but disappointingly, no reference to Peter Moser. The map drawn up twenty years later had a practical, scientific look about it and Tibby spotted John Moser's name written above a large property at the Kirkland end of the main street.

A bearded gentleman looked up from his scribbled notes and began to relate the story of his forebears to the room at large, striking the table repeatedly with his fist. The other researchers exchanged looks of disgust and tutted in whispers. The attendant scurried out from behind her desk, finger pressed firmly to her lips. Tibby caught Lottie's eye and winked. She went over to sit with Lottie and in silence they waited for the staff to bring the J&P Moser solicitors' letter box Tibby had ordered.

The first document Tibby picked up was the will and testament of Isaac Thompson of Kirkland. Isabella's husband. Tibby was becoming quite an expert reader of wills and soon established the original version was drawn up in 1839 then revised with a codicil in 1841, Isaac's dear wife Isabella having died in the interim. Isaac appointed Peter Moser, his wife's nephew, as one of the executors. Isaac's assets were to be divided between his nephews and Isabella's. So he was a generous husband who treated Isabella's family as though they were his own.

Attached to the first page of the will was an inventory, of Isaac's clothes, (shirts, cotton and silk handkerchiefs, stockings, breeches, coats, waistcoats, singlets, plaid undercuts, cloaks, topcoat, capes, gaiters and hats), books (collections of sermons, Shakespeare, a German grammar, the Life of Edward Burrough, a London guide) and furniture.

Tibby shuffled through the other papers; a receipt for

cash paid by Isaac Thompson "for work done for the benefit of Kirkland, mending and removing and puddling the sykes"; Isaac's name on a list of those entitled to vote in borough elections because he owned property; a handbill advertising a general meeting to call on the government to abolish slavery in the British Colonies with Isaac named as one of the sponsors.

Finally Tibby took out the bundle of papers relating to Isabella's burial. She was to be buried in the parish churchyard; there was wine enough in the house but they would need to buy biscuits; Mary Hogg, the servant presumably, was to be provided with mourning and grooms were to be sent to collect Isaac's nephew, Edward Thompson, solicitor. Ah! So that was how the Moser boys came to be solicitors; Isabella's husband asked his nephew to take them on as trainees.

A record of the funeral expenses listed:

Isabella's good oak coffin with plate and gold letters	£2.0.0
Church dues and bills	£0.18.0
Four bearers	£1.0.0
Total	£3.18.0

And there was a note recording payment of thirty shillings to Mary Hogg, nurse, "for attending to Isabella Thompson and subsequent services". Tibby's eyes filled with tears as she sat quietly holding the little slip of paper on which Mary had made her mark.

Lying at the bottom of the box was a sepia photograph of a wedding dated August 1869. The group of twenty or so family members was gathered on a lawn against a backdrop of trees. The women wore voluminous white gowns and ruched headdresses, some with veils, and clutched parasols; the men were in long dark jackets and clutched top hats. There were a number of clerical collars on view. All hands were hidden inside white gloves.

Everyone appeared ultra-staid and sombre, except for one of the women who had a sweet look and one of the young men who was staring cheekily into the camera. The bride herself looked particularly sour, as though suffering from bad indigestion and a hangover after her hen-night.

Someone had recorded the names on the back of the picture, from which Tibby worked out the bride was one of John Moser's fourteen children. John himself was seated next to the bride. Tibby peered at the face of the frail old man with deep set eyes, a broad nose, high cheekbones, and somewhat demented demeanour.

Peter died long before the photo was taken which in a way was a relief, Tibby had already formed a clear picture of him and didn't want it disturbed. The lad sitting cross-legged and bored at John's feet must be John's youngest son. He was born the year Peter died. Tibby had a theory Peter's wife gave her husband's tiny bible to the new born baby. After that the trail went cold.

'What a day!' Tibby said as they joined the motorway for the journey home. 'I know things about Isabella I don't know about anyone else. I even know who laid out her body and how much her funeral cost.'

'I liked the envelope from Bolton,' Lottie said. 'The one with nothing but "John Moser Esq., Kendal" for an address, no street name or number!' She pulled into the fast lane to overtake two lorries locked in mortal combat. 'And Isaac paid for "puddling the sykes", whatever that means! He was a good man and a good husband. I wonder why he and Isabella took so long to get together. How old were they when they married?'

'Forty two. They had thirty six years together. That's not bad,' Tibby said.

'But they didn't have any children. That's a shame.'

'The question is, what am I going to do next?' Tibby said quickly. She sensed Lottie was on the point of telling her how much she'd missed by not having a husband and family. 'I can't imagine life without Paitsons and Mosers.'

'You don't have to give them up. It would be a pity to waste all that research.'

'You mean write it up?' Tibby had already considered this. 'I could do but who'd be interested? It's not as if Isabella and Peter were famous and there's nothing spectacular about their story.'

'I was thinking more in terms of fiction. Historical novel. Always popular.' Lottie flashed her lights at the car hogging the middle lane.

When she thought about it, Tibby realised that's what she'd been doing from the beginning. Providing a backdrop to the facts, which were pretty minimal, giving personalities to the characters and explaining why things happened the way they did.

'You'll need a villain and a victim and a smattering of sex and violence. And a happy ending of course.' Lottie's enthusiasm was growing. 'You don't need to tell the reader the whole truth. You can play about with the dates to fit the plot.'

Tibby protested. She didn't know if she could bear to alter the dates she'd spent so long trying to establish.

'Okay, so you could write a blow by blow account of the actual search as an appendix. You know. Like they do for natural history programmes, ten minutes at the end showing how difficult it was to shoot the film. The camera crew waits six months in dense mist then on the very last day a snow leopard appears.'

'You're full of ideas!' Tibby laughed. 'We'll have to work on it together.'

'We'll need a strong title, something with punch.'

'I'd rather keep it simple. Just call it *Isabella's Bible* or *Isabella's Book*. That's where it all began, with her bible.' Tibby watched the flow of headlights travelling in the opposite direction. 'And when we've finished writing Isabella's story, I'll pass the bible to the first Paitson I come across. That's what Isabella would have wanted.'

CHAPTER 23

1840

They wanted to put Isabella's bed near the fireplace so she would feel the warmth but she preferred to have it placed against the window. When the sun shone, which was not very often, the light fell on her counterpane and she made shadow pictures with her hands, like she did as a child. Stiff and misshapen from rheumatic gout, her hands were good for little else these days; she could no longer put on her own clothes nor hold a book for more than a few minutes, even lifting the spoon to her mouth left her exhausted.

Mary Hogg came with a bowl of warm water every morning and dressed Isabella, even though she spent the day lying on her bed, and dear Isaac sat beside her when she took her meals and fed her with his own hand or held the cup to her lips when she grew weary.

Isabella's hands might be weak but her eyes still served her well, open or closed. When they were open she looked through the window at a thin strip of sky and beneath it the houses on the opposite side of the street, with their sagging roofs pulled low over small, mean eyes; houses where Kirkland folk lived and worked and loved and quarrelled and raised children and fell ill and died, as Isabella herself was dying. Isaac could afford to buy a larger, more comfortable property in Kirkby Kendal but preferred to stay amongst the people with whom he was raised, and to use whatever money he could spare for their benefit.

When she closed her eyes, as she often chose to do, Isabella saw shafts of sunlight passing through the leaves of the giant sycamore to cast patterns on the rear wall of Rawridding farmhouse, patterns which shivered and danced in the breeze. If you climbed high up in the tree you could look out over the valley to the south, and to the fells rising behind the house to the north. Shadows chased each other over the land as white curls of cloud tumbled across the sky, and the stones and blades of grass glittered in the sun like scattered jewels.

The sound of Alice calling the fowl and Agnes playing in the yard and the bleating of lambs, drifted upwards to mingle with the singing of birds and the rustle of leaves. Isabella fell asleep listening to the music of these memories and when she woke, for the first few minutes she could not tell whether she was in Kirkland or Dentdale.

Mary Hogg came into the room all bustle and breathlessness.

''Tis just as well you're dressed, Mistress Isabella. Master Peter and his wife are here, quite unexpected. They've brought the little one to meet you!' Mary bent over Isabella and tucked the stray hairs back under her bonnet. 'I'll just rub your cheeks to put some colour into them. Can you lift your head a moment while I plump up the pillow? That's better!'

'What does she look like?' Isabella made a feeble attempt to smooth the counterpane.

'No different from any other baby, to speak the truth. But then I've never seen a baby that I'd call pleasing to the eye, though I told Peter she was beautiful to humour him. At least she doesn't look sickly and that's a relief. Now I'll just get rid of these breakfast pots then I think we are ready.'

Isabella heard Peter talking to someone downstairs, then two people climbed step by step until they reached the creaking boards of the first floor. They did not come in immediately but stood in the shadows whispering to each other.

Twitching with impatience, Isabella strained to see what it was delayed them. Supposing she died right now, without ever setting eyes on the little girl? She called out but her voice dissipated before it had travelled halfway

221

across the room.

Now they were coming towards her; Peter, so smart in his frock-coat and trousers and Mary Elizabeth with her golden hair tied at the nape of her neck in the modern way which Isabella thought severe and unflattering. Peter bent to kiss Isabella's cheek, then took the priceless bundle from his wife's arms and laid it between two carefully positioned bolsters before pulling back the shawl to reveal a tiny face.

'Aunt Isabella, may I introduce my beautiful daughter. She's called Mary Elizabeth like her mother, but she will be known to the family as Beth. She's drawn breath for barely eight weeks while you have lived almost eighty years!' Peter freed one of the new-born fists from the shawl and curled it round Isabella's finger. 'Dr Turner is pleased with her progress. Just see how strong she is!'

Isabella looked at the tightly shut eyes, the pursed lips sucking at an imaginary nipple, the soft cheeks and firm chin, and could scarcely believe what she saw was real. Mary Elizabeth's womb had quickened six times since her marriage, only to expel its contents before the infant was fully formed.

And each time the light in her eyes became duller and her mouth smiled a little less, and seeing his wife dejected, Peter's heart grew twice as heavy. And now here she was, Peter's daughter, Isabella's granddaughter, gripping Isabella's finger and snuffling and wriggling and very much alive.

'I think she's on the verge of wakening,' Mary Elizabeth said, pleased to have an excuse to retrieve the bundle. 'Let me take her lest she disturb you with her cries.'

At the sound of her mother's voice, the infant opened her eyes which were deep purple and brimming with wisdom, as if they saw everything there is to see and what is more, understood it.

'Yes, take her before she grows fretful.' Isabella kissed the tiny forehead. 'Thank you for bringing her. Now please excuse me, I'm very tired.'

When Mary came up later she found the mistress in a sleep from which she could not be roused. The doctor said nothing more could be done, so Isaac sat beside Isabella and watched the rise and fall of her breathing gradually diminish until, two days later, the movement ceased altogether.

For local history I have relied heavily on:

Bingham, Roger, *Kendal - A Social History* (Cicerone Press: Milnthorpe, 1995)

Satchell, John, *Kendal on Tenterhooks* (Kendal Civic Society & Frank Peters Publishing: Kendal, 1984)

Satchell, John, *The Kendal Weaver* (Kendal Civic Society & Frank Peters Publishing: Kendal, 1986)

White, Andrew, *Kendal: A History* (Carnegie Publishing: Lancaster, 2013)

ABOUT THE AUTHOR

Alison Mukherjee was born in Scotland, grew up in England and has lived and worked in India. She taught Religious Studies in schools and Higher Education establishments and was employed as a social work practitioner and educator. She lives with her husband in the Midlands.

Made in the USA
Charleston, SC
25 May 2016